All That Glitters

All That Glitters

K.M. PEYTON

Forelock Books

Published by Forelock Books Ltd.

Beaglejack Barn, Blackgate Lane, Pulborough,
West Sussex. RH20 1DD

www.forelock-books.co.uk

First published in 2014

Printed in the EU on behalf of Latitude Press Ltd.

A CIP catalogue record for this book is available from the British Library

ISBN 978-0-9928-7080-5

To my good friend Sue Howard,
an expert in DressARGE.

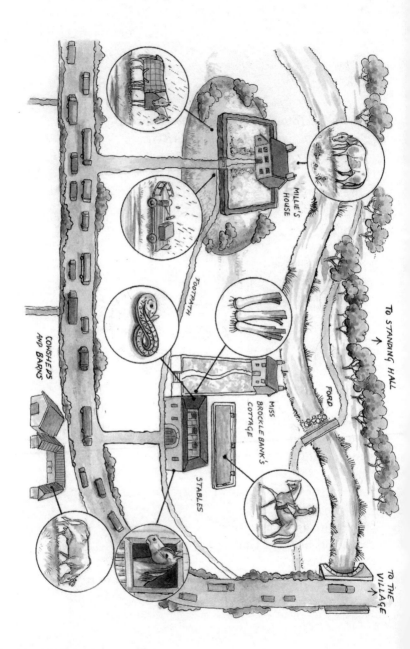

COWSHEDS AND BARNS

MILLIE'S HOUSE

FOOTPATH

MISS BROCKLE BANK'S COTTAGE

STABLES

FORD

TO STANDING HALL

TO THE VILLAGE

Chapter 1

'Tummy Creambun lost her gold bracelet when she was mucking out and asked me to ask you if you could find it with your metal detector.'

Millie Hodge appealed to the better nature of her brother Jake without much hope.

'What, in all that horse poo?'

'In the straw.'

'Yuck.'

'Why on earth can't you call that girl by her proper name? Tummy indeed! How would you like it?' Millie's mother demanded.

'Her real name is Autumn Greenbaum and her sister is called Bumble Bee Greenbaum, so we call them Tummy and Bummy Creambun. They don't mind. They laugh.'

'God in heaven, what were their parents thinking of?'

Their mother, Susan, found it hard to come to terms with current names – Zak, India, Brooklyn, Jade and suchlike – and had thought herself daring to call her daughter Millie thirteen years ago. Whatever next?

'Their parents are professors.'

'Professors of what? Flora and fauna presumably?'

'No. Psychiatry.'

'That explains it.'

Millie wasn't sure what it explained. Certainly the Greenbaum parents were pretty loopy but whose weren't? Hers were dinosaurs, dug up from times past. They wore waxed jackets for best and their only outings were to the cattle market and occasionally --- big deal! --- to an agricultural show. Their living was breeding beef cattle, so perhaps it was understandable, but Millie thought there was a life beyond cows. Her best friend Imogen's parents were in advertising and were forever going to New York and Paris and Singapore which was so glamorous, but when Imogen came to stay she said she wished her parents were farmers and stayed at home a bit more often. No pleasing anybody really.

'It's only pizza and chips. I've only just got in from the calves.'

They sat down at the table, not waiting for their father. No good feeding him pizza in any case. He reared beef and ate beef, and having pizza set before him would send him off into one of his frequent rages. To Millie and Jake, pizza was a treat.

'Will you look for it?' Millie persisted to Jake. 'She says if her mother finds out she was wearing it in the stables she'll go potty. She said she'd give you a fiver if you find it.'

'I could go down after tea.' Grudgingly.

It wasn't very far, after all. The stables were only a field away, downhill towards the river. They belonged to Miss Brocklebank, a rather weird lady who lived in what was once a farm labourer's cottage adjoining the stable yard. Millie spent a good deal of her spare time there with her friend Imogen who kept her pony at livery with Miss Brocklebank, along with the Creambuns. Calling the old dump a livery yard was somewhat ambitious: there were only the three ponies in the decrepit yard and no facilities. No arena, no floodlights for evening riding, no smart horseboxes in the non-existent parking space ... nothing like the elegant Equestrian Centre on the other side of town. The 'town' was really a village, but everyone around talked of going into town, not to the village. If only! ... Millie and Imogen always thought, marooned deep in the country with only one bus an hour to the bright lights, and the last one back at twenty-one thirty.

'Don't waste time down there. You've your homework to do.'

The same old mantra ringing in their ears, they snatched their jackets and set off over the stile out of their backyard and down the field. Their house stood on a knoll and looked down to the river at the back and down to the very busy road at the front. Beyond Miss Brocklebank's stable yard the road and the river converged at the bridge into the village. The village sign stood up proudly: 'You are now entering Under Standing', to which some joker had sprayed in black letters 'Mis' to join up with Under. Their path down the hill was well worn, for they both used Miss Brocklebank's stables as a sort of den, a private place to hang out with their friends, Millie with Imogen and Jake with his mate Harry. It was a refuge from their father's bad temper, and there was a small tack room with a sofa in it and an electric kettle and nobody came, save the Creambuns, who didn't matter. Miss Brocklebank never came. She was always working in her garden.

'You must admit,' Millie said, as they came down the hill, 'her garden is stunning.'

The best view of it was from where they were now, on the footpath going down the hill. The garden lay at the bottom, bounded on the far side by the end wall of the stable yard.

'I don't suppose she ever gets this view of it. She never comes up to the farm.'

'Thank goodness.'

'Oh, she's all right. Just crazy, that's all.'

The garden was a riot of dahlias, exotic daisies and spiky oriental things, cabbages and leeks and tomatoes all mixed up with delphiniums and lupins and roses and plants unknown, even to Miss Brocklebank. She visited stately homes and came back with pocketsful of cuttings and seedlings.

'It's all for the cause. They don't miss these little things.'

Her cottage at the bottom beside the river was obviously lacking the care lavished on the garden. It was old and decrepit and showed no signs of being loved. One of the upstairs windows was broken and patched with cardboard, and all the paintwork was peeling. She lived there alone, a source of worry to the children's mother who considered her 'strong, but not really capable'. She meant in the top storey. The children liked her because she never interfered with what they were doing, allowing them the run of her stable yard.

Jake and Millie's path led to the boundary of her garden, round the top end of it, and to the door in the high wall of the old stable yard. Jake pushed it open and revealed the familiar cosy square of old buildings. Imogen's bike was flung down in the middle of the yard.

Jake, grumpy, said, 'Where then?'

'You know where the Creambun ponies are: in the end box, the big one.'

They lived together, a pair, like their owners. They were hairy and brown, said to be Dartmoors, and were called Dodo and Duffer.

Only one wing of the old yard was given over to stables, the other three sides, apart from a section used as a hay and straw store, were filled with the junk of ages past, mainly old machinery and carts. In the wing opposite the stables was a large archway which gave on to the drive which led out to the main road. But they none of them rode out this way any more: the traffic was too bad. They had to go round the back by the river.

Luckily the Creambun box was empty. The ponies were out in the field and as there was no sign of Imogen, Millie supposed she had gone for a ride, a quick one round the fields before it got dark. Jake humped his machine down to the empty box and Millie sat on the feed-bin, drumming her heels, waiting for Imogen.

Millie longed to have a pony but her father said yes, okay, if it lived across the road with the cattle: he wasn't paying the Bonkers Brocklebank for livery. But what good was that, separated from her friend by the ghastly uncrossable road so that they were unable to ride together? He seemed prepared to let her face its horrors, when the main cause of his bad temper was the road. He had to cross it with the tractor several times a day to get to his cattle sheds and had to wait ages for a gap to go across. The road was awful. The village was full of notices shouting 'Bypass Now!' 'Peace for Under Standing!' Although the Creambuns and Imogen came from the village by bike, they always cycled across the field from the bridge. Even now, in the stable, Millie could hear the constant hum of the rush-hour traffic from away down the drive.

When the stables were built a couple of centuries back the road must have been a sleepy lane. Millie loved the feel of them, their 'oldness', as if they had grown out of the water meadows that surrounded them. The walls still bore the ancient mangers and wooden hayracks where generations of gentle cart horses had come home to feed every night, and the brick floors had been worn by their great hooves into a pattern of grooves. But the end box where Jake was starting up his metal detector had only an earth floor; it must once have been a feed shed or harness room. Jake was already complaining about the pong. Millie took no notice. She loved the smell of the ponies and sat picturing her own, stabled happily next to Imogen's Barney. Why was her father so mean? You could get one for almost nothing these days. It wasn't as if they were poor, as far as she knew: his beautiful Aberdeen Anguses were bought by Waitrose, only the best. She supposed she and Jake were something of a disappointment to him, Jake showing no signs at all of wanting to be a farmer, and herself a bit of a dream, not the sort of sturdy girl in a white overall helping him at shows. Even the calves got away from her and knocked the judge flying. Her father didn't ask her to help any more. Children who were her own age or younger got rosettes for handling. Her father would have been proud of her, might even have bought her a pony, if she had been more inclined to cows. Or so she thought.

She slipped off the feed-bin and went out to see what Imogen was doing. There was an old barn door at the end of the stable row where they could go in and out on the river into Miss Brocklebank's fields. They were water meadows that stretched all the way to the village – 'full of weeds, disgraceful,' according to Mr Hodge, but rather nice to Millie's mind, the river's edge lined with bulrushes and meadowsweet, the top end full of buttercups. The river flooded quite often in the winter and sometimes the water came right up to the stable yard and into Miss Brocklebank's kitchen, but so far it had done little damage. It had never come up her stairs. The image of Miss Brocklebank sitting on her roof in her flannel pyjamas awaiting rescue was rather delicious but so far only a figment of the imagination.

Imogen was coming up the field carrying her saddle and bridle. The ponies were still living out and she had turned Barney away with the two Dartmoors. In spite of her parents being lovely and rich and indulging their only daughter largely with whatever she wanted, Imogen had chosen a very manky pony from the horse rescue to call her own. Barney, even now he was well fed and groomed, still looked what he was: a poorly bred cross of dubious parents probably from traveller origins. At least he was all one colour, a rather washy bay. But he had a very sweet and affectionate nature and big faithful eyes and tried his best to please. As Imogen said, 'I just want a friend. Not a winner.' Millie reckoned Barney was a winner, getting Imogen.

'Hi.'

They stood and watched the pony moving away in the dusk to join the other two. There was a beautiful purplish-red sunset happening beyond the water meadows and both girls were quite happy looking at it at that moment, forgetting everything else. For a minute or two.

Then: 'I've got masses of homework,' Imogen said. 'I must go home.'

They started back to the stable yard. Imogen was very clever and would no doubt knock off her masses of homework in no time, Millie thought. Unlike herself, a plodder. She got there in the end but it took her twice as long as it took Imogen. Ah well. They went to the same local school but Imogen was one year higher.

'What on earth's Jake doing in the Creambuns' box?'

'The bracelet Tummy lost – remember? He gets a five-pound reward if he finds it.'

The machine was still whirring. They went to the end and looked in.

'Have you got it?'

'Yes. It didn't take a minute.'

'Why are you still at it then?'

'Well, listen. It's going crazy down in this corner. There must be something else.'

'Old bucket,' said Imogen.

'Old horseshoe,' said Millie.

'Is there a spade around? I'd like to dig and see.'

'You can't dig a hole in the ponies' box!'

'I'll put it back. Why don't you go and lose yourselves?'

They laughed. What an idiot!

'All he ever gets is horseshoes and the odd spanner or dog-chain or nails and things. Just rubbish.'

'Yes, but one day – who knows? I can see the attraction,' Imogen said.

'He saved up for ages for it. But after the first novelty wore off and he never found anything he got fed up with it.'

They went out into the dusk and Imogen picked up her bike.

'Perhaps it's one of these down there. A Roman bicycle.' Imogen laughed.

'See you tomorrow.'

Millie didn't wait for Jake but plodded back up the hill.

At least Jake had earned himself a fiver.

Millie was going to bed by the time Jake came up. Surprisingly, he came into her room after a loud knock and a shout: 'You decent?'

'What is it?'

Millie was standing at the window. Her bedroom was at the back and looked down to the river, a much better view than Jake's room at the front which looked towards the main road. Millie always looked out before she went to bed and when she got up, to see how the day was. She loved the river. She was standing there wishing she had a pony and could go riding with Imogen, the two of them together. If you crossed the river by the ford behind the stables you could ride for miles over the fields and through the woods on the other side. It would be lovely, the two of them. Once she had tried borrowing Dodo but Dodo wouldn't go anywhere without Duffer and the trip had been a disaster.

She said to Jake, 'I hope you didn't dig a big hole in the ponies' box.'

'No. Only a bit and I put it back. But look, look what was there.'

He held out his hand.

It wasn't like Jake to be so confiding, and Millie recognised a tremor of excitement in his voice. She looked at what he was holding. It was quite small, an S-shaped snake in what appeared to be bronze, minutely engraved all down its back with a pattern of what looked like flowers and leaves. But engrained earth made it difficult to see exactly.

'What is it?'

'I think it's a clasp of some sort. It's very old, I'm sure. Really old.'

Millie took it and tried to rub some of the earth away.

'Put it under the bathroom tap, get rid of the soil, then we might see. Did you show it to Mum?'

'No. It's a secret. I don't want anyone to know. The machine was going like fury even after I took this out so who knows what else is there?'

8

'Perhaps—'

It was everyone's dream, hoovering away with their detectors, to find hidden treasure. Like winning the lottery. Millie could see the attraction. They cleaned it with a nailbrush and examined it minutely.

'Look, I think it had a jewelled eye. There's a little hole there where the jewel has fallen out.'

'And there is a bit on the back – look – that could have been a pin, but it's broken. Like it was a clasp for a cloak or something.'

'It's lovely,' Millie said. 'You ought to show it to—'

'No! Don't be stupid! We don't want anyone else butting in. I only showed you because you and Imogen are always down there and I can't keep it a secret from you. But there's more stuff there, I'm sure, the way the machine was juddering away, and it's mine. I found it. You mustn't tell anyone! It might be a fortune.'

Millie could see his point.

'But you can't go digging away under there, the whole wall might cave in! And what about the Creambuns?'

'There's lots of room at the other end. They can move their stupid ponies down past Barney's box.'

Millie could see all sorts of arguments against Jake's declaration but decided not to list them. Not yet.

'If the treasure is under the end wall, most of it's probably outside under Miss Brocklebank's prize Brussels sprouts. If it's mediaeval or Roman or whatever, the stable yard wouldn't have been there then.'

'Damn, what if it's under her garden!'

'Even if it's worth a million, she'd never let you dig up her garden.'

'At night, when she's in bed—'

'Like body-snatchers! It might be a grave!'

They got a bit silly, picturing Miss Brocklebank coming out in her pyjamas with a torch while they hid under the purple sprouting broccoli, but they both felt excited by the find, Millie now as well as Jake. The little serpent she held in her hand was heavy and undoubtedly old and beautifully crafted.

'It's the real thing, I'm sure you're right.'

'But promise you won't tell!'

'No, of course I won't.'

'I'll tell Harry. I can trust him. I suppose Imogen will have to know. But no one else. No one at all.'

'No.'

Jake went back to his room with his treasure and Millie went to bed and lay in the dark imagining her brother becoming a millionaire and the television at the door and her father being all sweetness and light and their pictures in the newspaper.

But she knew those things only happened to other people. Despite the little serpent, it was probably only a dead bucket under there.

Chapter 2

Millie got out of bed the next morning and looked out of the window down to the river. She always slept with the curtains drawn back and always got out of bed on the window side and looked out, a matter of habit, even when still half asleep. It was a nice view, after all, and its contemplation got her brain gently whirring: what day was it? What was happening? Could she remember where she had left her trainers last night? Would Imogen remember to bring her that book she promised? Millie did not spring into action like her brother Jake. She considered it first.

She never saw any movement in her view. The cattle were on the other side of the house and there was nothing in the steep field down to the river. Nothing on the other side either to disturb the softly rolling fields and woods. The river, wide and gentle, curled round the knoll their house stood on, made its lazy way past Miss Brocklebank's cottage, round her fields and disappeared under the village bridge.

Like a picture postcard. Nice. Millie stood looking.

However, for once something was moving down there. Millie blinked. A pony! Not one of theirs: it was whitish, greyish in patches, a faded piebald, standing on the edge of the river at the bottom of the field. Amazing! Millie, who longed to have a pony of her own, thought in her dozy waking moments that perhaps her prayers had been answered. It was abandoned, she thought. No one wants it!

I want it!

She came sharply awake, determined. Catch it before her father sees it! Catch it before anyone sees it. It's for me. It's mine!

She scrambled into her clothes and ran downstairs. Her father was away across the road and her mother still dressing upstairs. She grabbed her dirty stable jacket and let herself out quietly. The morning was sharp and the grass heavy with dew. She hurried through her mother's garden (nothing like Miss Brocklebank's), squirmed under the barbed wire fence then ran and slithered down the hill, gasping with excitement. The pony was not disturbed by her appearance. It was grazing on the edge of the river and scarcely bothered to look up as Millie panted into view. It trailed a frayed rope which was fastened roughly round its neck; there was no headcollar. Travellers' pony, Millie thought: both its colour and its condition suggested it. Although it was spring and the new grass full of goodness, it was thin, its ribs showing, and its coat still had lumps of shaggy winter hair unshed. It was far removed from a dream pony.

But Millie dismissed these initial observations in her excitement.

If it had been a dream pony, anxious owners would be scouring the countryside. This one was likely abandoned and, if not, was hardly the sort its owners would take much trouble searching for, for at close quarters it was in really bad condition, its coat mangy, a bloody cut over one eye and a swollen off foreleg. It made no effort to avoid being caught. It just threw up its head from the grazing and looked without much curiosity at the approaching human being.

Millie took the frayed rope, her mind racing. She must take it to the stable yard and hide it there before anyone saw it. Not a difficult proposition as they only had to walk along by the river and up round Miss Brocklebank's garden to get there. She set off and the pony came with her without too much persuasion, obviously used to doing as it was told.

Millie talked to it and laid her hand over its mud-caked mane. It was a colour known as blue and white, about thirteen hands high and – sadly – rather in the Barney mode: ill-bred and unhandsome. But, like Barney, it had (she could tell already) a nice nature and large, trusting eyes. What it had, from the look of it, to be trusting about, Millie could not guess. But she loved it immediately. As they walked along she thought of a name for it: Bluebell. It just came into her head without her trying and she accepted it, soppy as it was. Bluebell and Barney.

They were a pair. Millie was so happy she wanted to dance and sing. She did both as she made her way to the stables and Bluebell came obediently, no doubt wondering what sort of a mad person had taken him over.

The other ponies were still out in the field and the stable yard was deserted. Millie decided to put the pony into Dodo and Duffer's box as it was the only one ready, and it was large and comfortable. Jake had filled in his hole as promised and there was plenty of fresh straw which Bluebell started to eat immediately. Millie fetched a large slice of hay and filled the water bucket to the top and cut off the rope loop.

'There, aren't you a lucky boy! Or girl?' She hadn't noticed which.

She looked and saw that it was male, which made Bluebell rather an unfortunate name, but her mind refused to change it.

'Poor Bluebell.'

Much as she wanted to stay, Millie knew it would be wise to hurry home and pretend nothing had happened. Bluebell was a secret. Nobody must know, not yet. She remembered Jake had a secret too, and they were both in the same loose box. Suppose? Suppose …

She ran back up the hill, got her breath back, then walked into the kitchen calmly as if she had just come downstairs. No one noticed she had been out, her mother preoccupied with marmalade making and Jake with his hidden treasure.

When they left for school together, Millie told him about Bluebell. He wasn't all that interested, except could she move him tonight as he wanted to have another go with his detector.

'When you think about it, the stable yard is pretty old. There must have been a whole farm down there once, and Miss Brocklebank's house is called Villa Cottage. It could well have Roman connotations. Before the road, it's where the river is fordable … It all makes sense. It could be a Roman site.'

Millie agreed, although she felt very sceptical. But she could see that the possibilities were burning in Jake's brainbox.

'Pity Miss Brocklebank's garden is where it is though,' she said. 'If your machine goes mad there you'll never be able to dig for it.'

'No. It's a bummer.'

They caught the school bus, which stopped to pick them up at the bottom of their drive. Millie couldn't wait to tell Imogen about her find and get back to the stables after school. Imogen, as was to be expected, was thrilled: the find was far more exciting than Jake's snake.

'I bet there's nothing else there of value, just the usual old bit of trough or a horseshoe. I can't wait to see Bluebell That's a terrible name, by the way.'

But it was stuck.

'No worse than Barney. Proper horses today have German names with letters and numbers on the end, like aeroplanes. It's disgusting.'

'Yes, for shows. But at home they're called Harry and Tommy and things.'

As soon as school was over the two girls rushed off across the fields to the stable yard. They usually went home first and came back after tea, but Imogen couldn't wait to see Bluebell and Millie was terrified someone might have taken him away.

But all was well. The pony was happily devouring what was left of his bedding and when Millie opened the door he looked up and she saw his nose quiver into a soft whicker of greeting.

'Look, he loves me! Look, Imogen, isn't he beautiful?'

Imogen looked and said, 'No, not really,' and laughed, but Millie could see she was thrilled too.

'We'll be able to ride together. If you can keep him, that is. His owners might turn up, or your father might not let you.'

But Millie was optimistic. 'We'll keep him hidden in here for a few days in case anyone comes looking down the river.' She chose not to think about her father.

'He might not look so bad when he's cleaned up.'

'Let's come back after tea. And I'll bring Barney in tonight to keep him company.'

It was a beautiful evening, and Friday, so no homework to bother with, and so Millie went leaping down the hill after tea to meet Imogen again. Jake wouldn't be able to come, thank goodness, as he had been collared by one of the teachers to take part in making a film about global warming.

'He knows about cameras and things,' Millie explained to Imogen, 'Not much about global warming though.' But enough to keep him nicely out of their way. Imogen fetched Barney in from the field and put him in his loose-box and went to study Bluebell.

'Blimey,' she said.

'What do you mean, blimey?'

'Well, he's not exactly red rosette material, is he?'

'No more than is Barney and you *chose* him. This one just walked in.'

'True.'

'They make a good pair. Manky and all wrong, but the same size and shape.'

'Bad shape.'

'Yes, but nice.'

'Wonky but nice.'

They then proceeded to get the giggles, easily done.

'Bluebell! I ask you! Wonky would be a good name.'

'Only if you change Barney to Manky.'

'Manky and Wonky!'

'Sounds like a circus act. We could teach them tricks!'

'We could enter for that class at the Standing show, the one the Equestrian Centre always wins – you know, going round in circles together and trotting sideways and that stuff. The Manky and Wonky Quadrille.'

'A quadrille is four, stupid.'

'Duo, then.'

In spite of the jokes, Millie had a pang at remembering the beautiful ponies that won the Riding Quadrille, miniature thoroughbreds with elegantly arched necks and pointed toes, moving like clockwork, smooth as silk. Dream ponies. Bluebell stood before her hairy and bony, looking at her with expectant eyes. She put her arms round his neck and gave him a cuddle. He smelled lovely.

'My dream pony!'

Imogen got out her grooming tools and they set to on Bluebell, one on each side, taking off the top dirt. He stood quietly, tied to the door of Barney's box, so that he could talk to Barney if he wanted. Barney had introduced himself with some eye-rolling and snorting, but now they were friendly, their two plain heads nose to nose.

'Really he needs a bath,' Imogen said.

'We'll give him a bath tomorrow. I'll just wash his mane and tail for now.'

The stables were in a row inside the barn. Once they had been stalls with the horses tied up, but now with bars fixed across the ends they had been turned into loose-boxes. The stalls had been quite generously sized, for large cart horses, so the boxes were a fair size. Even with Bluebell newly installed next to Barney and the Dartmoors, there were still six empty places. Miss Brocklebank had always been going to run a proper livery yard, but what with all the work in her garden she never seemed to have got round to it.

Imogen said, 'My ma says Miss Brocklebank's got a niece coming to live with her. She heard in the newspaper shop.'

'Poor niece! But mum's always said Miss Brocklebank needs looking after. My mum will be pleased.'

'As long as she doesn't interfere down here.'

'No, we don't want that.'

'She's probably as dopey as Miss Brocklebank. If she's volunteering to live with her she must be mad.'

'Probably another gardener.'

What neither of them wanted to talk about was whether Millie's father would allow her to keep Bluebell. Now the pony was clean and tidy and his thick tail was white instead of khaki-coloured, he looked quite respectable, and his docile, trusting nature was endearing. He had made no attempt to bite or complain even when they had brushed his most ticklish place. Millie was falling in love fast.

After some thought Imogen said, 'Even if your father doesn't want you keep him, what will he do? He can't just turn him out again.'

'No he can't. I think he was just abandoned. He escaped his

tether and no one has been looking for him. Dad might let me keep him with the cows, at least, and then I'll just have to think of something.'

'Perhaps you should ask the police if he's been reported missing.'

'Yes, and suppose he has? I'm keeping quiet.'

'They certainly didn't look after him very well, whoever they were.'

Imogen was quite surprised by Millie's spark of determination to flout the law. Millie was really quite boringly good. Imogen was by nature disobedient and scornful. She got into a lot of trouble at school but because she was so outstandingly clever the school went to great lengths to humour her. If as expected she won a scholarship to Oxford or Cambridge without even trying they would take all the credit. Naturally she was not very popular. She took her friendship with Millie for granted, thrown together as they were in Miss Brocklebank's stables, but occasionally, as now, it surprised her and she realised that Millie was really the only friend she had. An unfamiliar spark of loyalty prompted her to say, 'If I hear anyone enquiring about a lost pony, I'll put them off the scent. I'll say we saw a pony on the other side of the main road, going away from the village.'

'Yeah, good.'

'It would be nice if we could ride together, after all.'

Having spruced up Bluebell, they mucked out the stables to put the ponies back. Jake's idea of filling up the hole he had dug was pretty sketchy and Millie fetched a spade to improve the job. He had made quite an effort in a short time and Millie could not help thinking of his terrier-like impatience to find treasure … was it really likely that there was anything there? She pushed the spade hard down into the disturbed earth hoping to find a horseshoe and so put him out of his misery and brought it up carefully to examine the soil. Certainly no horseshoe, but she could see the fascination that possessed Jake as she sifted through the spadeful with her fingers. Treasure trove! Finders, keepers, she understood was the rule, only to be shared with the person who owned the land. Oh, to be filthy rich, what fun! No wonder Jake was so hypnotised by his toy's conversation.

There was something small and hard in her handful. She picked it out, a coin, very small. Black. She supposed it was a farthing, although she had never seen one, only heard of them. A quarter of a penny. Her mother remembered her granny using them. They weren't worth anything: bad luck, Jake! She put it in her pocket and shovelled the soil back, stamping it hard. Perhaps her farthing was something more ancient … she would give it to Jake when she got home, just in case. Better than nothing, anyhow. She put a straw bed down and led the patient Bluebell back into his home. He would have to be hidden indoors for a while. Later, when nobody had claimed him, she would turn him out with the others.

'He likes being next to Barney. We'll get the Creambuns to stable Duffer and Dodo at the other end. If Jake wants to go on with his digging, he can rig up a big box for them.'

'I've just thought,' Imogen said, 'about riding him. How do you know he's broken in? He might be too young.'

'Yes, he might. Oh dear. How do you tell?'

'By their teeth.'

'How by their teeth?'

'I dunno. It's in books. I'll look it up.'

Imogen went out for her bike and Millie turned up the hill for home. The day had been amazing: her head was zinging. Her own pony! She just *knew* no one was going to come looking. He had come to find her, her own Bluebell!

Her father had come in and was taking his boots off in the kitchen and her mother was getting his dinner out of the oven. Millie wasn't going to say anything about the pony, not yet. Not until she had time to think things through, to think of a plan. Her mother might help her, if her father proved difficult.

But her mother was on to the other news of the day.

'Miss Brocklebank's got her niece coming to live with her. What a relief! She's not safe in that house on her own. She leaves the gas on all the time and won't throw her newspapers away. Her kitchen's piled high with them.'

'Not that spoilt brat from London, the one with all the money?'

'Yes, I think so. The one that married very young, divorced a year later and came away with a fortune. What she's going to make of Miss Brocklebank's cottage, heaven alone knows.'

'Well, they say Miss Brocklebank is very rich. I daresay now the old girl's on her last legs Miss Golddigger is coming to suck up to her, get her snout in the trough.'

'Perhaps. Perhaps she's come to persuade her to move into a decent bungalow in the village. That would be the best thing. But she'll never leave her garden, so that's a non-starter.'

'The whole place should be demolished. It's a dump. And the land is worthless, given to flooding.'

Millie could see that it was no moment to raise the subject of Bluebell. Everything was rubbish. Her father was often like that.

'Her garden is beautiful. She wins everything in the village show. Her leeks are always first, even when those men try their hardest to beat her.'

The leek patch was right against the stable wall where Jake was convinced the treasure trove lay. Millie thought, if she had problems, Jake's were bigger. There was no way he could dig there.

Later, when he had come in and they were watching television together, she remembered the farthing, and went and fished it out of her jacket pocket.

'There you are, treasure trove. A farthing.'

He took it.

'It's too thin for a farthing.'

'What is it then?'

'Dunno. I'll go and give it a scrub.'

He left the television, so he must have been interested. Half an hour later he came back. He flumped down on the sofa and

Millie could feel the electricity of excitement under the cushions.

'It's Roman!' he said in a quivering voice.

'Wow! Really?'

'Yes, I'm sure. It's got a Roman head on it, in a helmet.'

'Wow!'

But afterwards all Millie could think of was Miss Brocklebank's leeks.

Chapter 3

'We must be nearly there. This is the village, Under Standing, and it's the first right turn out of the village, over the bridge.'

Polly Power, driving her red Aston Martin (far too fast), spoke to her passenger, the glum young man beside her. He did not reply.

'Look, if you don't want to do this, say so,' she said, with some asperity. 'Throw it all in. Lose half a million bucks. I don't care. She's not asking much of you, your old granny, in exchange for all her money.'

The young man groaned.

'We've had this conversation before. I agreed. End of story.'

'Well, if you're going to be so damned miserable about it, and make everyone around you miserable, I'll be the one to opt out. So watch it.'

'Okay. Okay. Understood. Or should I say Under Standing?'

Polly laughed, a well-bred cackle.

'Funny name. The traffic's awful. No wonder there's all these notices: Bypass Now. Should've been ten years ago. Here's the bridge. Start looking for the drive. I'll need to indicate in good time.'

'It's coming up now. You can see the yard across the field, by the river. A good way off the road. Looks like a dump.'

'It is a dump. I know what I'm taking on, rest assured. Auntie's never touched it since her parents died. All she cares about is her garden, winning the leek class in the village show, and the best rose, all that sort of thing.'

She came to a halt, waiting for a gap in the oncoming traffic.

'Lucky I've got the money to spend on it.'

'You're a vulture, getting that pay-off from poor old Nick.'

'He could afford it!'

'You got your million far more easily than I'm ever going to get mine.'

'Rubbish. You earning yours is a doddle if you just put your addled mind to it.

You might even enjoy it once you get started.'

'Pigs might fly.'

The car turned at last and bumped its way up the rarely used drive. The big archway of the stable yard reared ahead.

'It must have been fine once. Splendid gateway. What a crime to let it run down like this.'

Polly drove her car into the yard, narrowly avoiding a bicycle thrown down in the middle.

'Auntie says she runs it as a livery yard. Let's see what the punters' horses are like. They can't be very ambitious coming to a dump like this, especially when there's the Standing District Equestrian Centre down the road.

Millie and Imogen had seen the car come through the archway and had already guessed who it was. They were in Bluebell's box, about to give him another groom. Millie grabbed Imogen's arm and pulled her down into the corner of the box on the same side as the door where they were unlikely to be seen. Why she did this she never quite knew, save that she was scared of what she had heard of the money-grubbing divorcee and acted in a sort of panic. Imogen squeaked and pulled away but Millie hissed at her to shut up.

'It's *her*!'

Imogen immediately wriggled round and put her eye to a large crack in the wooden wall of the box.

'Cor!'

She got an eyeful of black boots, leather trousers, a biker jacket, wrists covered in bracelets, bright red fingernails, honey blonde hair and flashing inquisitive eyes casting all around with an expression of sneering distaste. Behind her, so that Imogen couldn't really see him, was what appeared to be a tall young man.

'Who's he?' she whispered.

Millie couldn't see anything other than Bluebell's tummy. Friendly as always he moved over to greet the newcomers and Millie got a glimpse of an appalled face drawing back from his slobber, the lips uttering, 'Oh my God, what rubbish have we got here?'

'Hey, and this one too,' said the young man, looking into Barney's box. 'Looks like the rescue home here.'

At this Imogen leapt up shrieking, 'How dare you!'

Millie wanted to die.

The woman with the boots said, 'Who exactly are you, may I ask?'

Millie shrunk even further into the straw.

'I'm a livery owner. I belong here. I am a client of Miss Brocklebank's. And who are you, driving in here making insulting remarks about our ponies?'

'My name is Polly Power and I'm Miss Brocklebank's niece. I'm taking over the yard, so now you are a client of mine, not of Miss Brocklebank. So I think we had better be friends.'

She smiled a glacial smile and stuck out her hand to shake. Imogen, after a moment's hesitation, took it, and said, 'My friend is here too, Millie Hodge. This pony is hers.'

'What were you doing crawling about in there in the straw?'

'We were grooming Bluebell but we dropped the hoofpick and we were looking for it.'

How clever she was, Millie thought! She would have come clean and said they were eavesdropping.

'Where are the other horses then? Besides just these two –?'

'There aren't any. Only two little Dartmoors who live out mostly. Just us. We run the yard.'

'Really?'

Polly was somewhat stunned by this belligerent child and instead of saying, 'I'm sorry but I run the yard now and you can take a running jump,' as her instinct prompted her, she bit back the words and smiled ingratiatingly.

'Well, isn't that nice? I can see you will be a great help to me when I take over.'

Imogen, being equally tactful, swallowed down a scathing, 'Oh yeah?' and said, 'Does Miss Brocklebank know you're here?' (meaning go and see her and get out of our hair).

'Not yet. I'd better go down to the cottage and make myself known. She's expecting me for lunch.'

'Cripes,' said Imogen, seeing that Polly was a smoked salmon sort of person, and knowing that Miss Brocklebank lived on baked beans and cabbage.

Polly turned to the young man and said, 'You want to come? Or wait here?'

'I'll wait in the car,' he said.

'I might be a while.'

'It's okay. I'll read the paper.'

They both departed, leaving Millie and Imogen stunned.

'Blimey, she's horrible!'

They could both see their cosy world collapsing in tatters.

'She'll chuck us out! Or put the price up sky-high. You can see we're not the sort of livery people she wants.'

'Perhaps Miss Brocklebank won't like her. She's not her sort of person.'

'No, but she's the sort of person who gets her own way. Poor Miss Brocklebank won't stand a chance.'

'And who's he, the sulky one? She didn't introduce us. Is he her new guy?'

'He didn't look very loving.'

'No, he looked hating.'

'Perhaps we should suss him out.'

They went to the cobwebby window that looked out on to the yard and peered through. The young man was standing with his hands in his pockets morosely kicking the front wheel of the Aston Martin.

'Not a happy bunny.'

'We could offer him a cup of tea,' Millie suggested. 'Find out things.'

'Yes! He obviously doesn't like her, so he might be quite chatty.'

They had trouble making a mug clean enough to offer to a visitor but there were still a few dregs of long-life milk and some claggy sugar in a bag if he wanted it. Imogen went out and invited him to join them in elevenses.

'Okay,' he said, and came back into the stable. They both stared at him over their tea mugs. He was really quite dishy, dark and well groomed. Not their sort, but interesting.

'My name's Joe,' he said. 'You are—?'

They said.

'Are you her boyfriend?' Imogen asked boldly (rudely, Millie thought, blushing for her).

'Oh God, no. No fear. She teaches me. Dressage.'

'Oh, dressARGE,' Imogen said, the way they always said it. 'We're not into dressARGE. We're not clever enough. We just ride about, stop and go sort of thing.'

'She says anyone who rides at all does dressage, whatever. It's just obedience and control.'

'I thought it was riding sideways instead of straight on and going round in circles.'

Joe smiled (yes, rather nice!), 'There's quite a lot of that, true. I'm not that good. I'd rather ride straight on. Gallop, you know, have a bit of fun. But I'm not allowed.'

'Blimey!'

'She says anyone can gallop about.'

'Yes, but—' Imogen was stymied. Why did he do what he was told? 'Are you riding her horse then? Or something. Why can't you gallop about if you want to?'

'No. I've got my own horse. I have to do as I'm told because I'm working for something
... Oh, it's a very long story — '

'An exam? What?'

'No. Money, basically,' he said.

'Oh ...' Both Millie and Imogen groaned. Boring!

'All the same, if it's a very long story, we've got ages till Thingy comes back, so you can tell us. We need to know, if your horse is coming here. What's it like, by the way? Gorgeous?'

'Yes, very gorgeous. Have you got any biscuits? I'm starving.'

They got the jar and were lucky enough to find two grim-looking ginger biscuits in the bottom, which they offered.

'Sorry, that's all. The boys take them. We buy them and they eat them.'

'Boys? Are there many of you round here?'

'No. Only four. Six if you count Jake and his mate Harry.' Millie felt a sad stroke of loss at seeing Jake's plans for digging up his treasure going down the drain. 'Tell us your long story.'

'Not very long really. I've got a very rich grandmother and she's going to leave me all her money if I get off my backside and do something she thinks is manly. All I do is computers, you see, all day and all night. I service them all day as a living and play games on them all night for fun and she thinks this is a disgraceful way to live. So she's given me this rather splendid horse and says I've got to get out there and win a few silver cups or she'll leave all her money to the cats' home.'

The two girls digested this. They agreed with his grandmother that he must be a number one nerd to spend day and night with computers but couldn't quite see why he had to do dressage to prove he was manly.

'Can't you race him? Over jumps, of course. That's very manly.'

'He's not a thoroughbred. He's a warmblood. They don't race,

I'm told.'

'No, that's true.'

'It's not all that important what I do. It's just to make me get out and learn to ride a horse. She thinks – my grandmother, that is – that it will transform my life, to get outside and ride a horse. Wean me off computers. It's Polly – she's my cousin – who insists on dressage because it's her thing. She's got a fantastic dressage horse. She says I'd be a real fool to forgo the money, but I don't care really. I make plenty. But when Polly's after you, I can tell you, it's difficult to shake her off. And of course, having been given the horse, I had to get Polly's help because what do I know about horses? Nothing. I just asked her to look after it for me and now look what's happened …'

His voice trailed off. The two girls digested this information slowly. It had all sorts of implications. Two fantastic horses were going to come to their stable. Polly was someone who must be obeyed – although they had rather come to that conclusion without Joe's story. Joe was a nerd who was to be transformed by riding a horse in the great outdoors, which he rarely saw. (He was rather pale and wishy-washy and the great outdoors would certainly improve his quite promising looks.)

'And – a livery stable? Does she want lots of horses here?'

'Build it up, she said. Make money. She thinks a lot about money. Get all her friends here at a hundred pounds a week or something.'

Even Imogen couldn't think of anything to say at this, while Millie felt quite faint.

'What about Miss Brocklebank?'

But they knew that Miss Brocklebank hardly ever came into the stable yard. It was only her garden she cared about. And how could poor old Miss Brocklebank withstand her niece when it seemed nobody else could?

'Polly's got a lot of money from her divorce and is dying to spend it. She thinks this would be a fantastic place to take on.

And apparently the old auntie wants watching a bit these days. I daresay she's also got a load of money to leave to someone, so Polly's getting her nose in there as well.'

Millie remembered that's what her father said. Her snout in the trough.

'She sounds a right cow,' Imogen said.

They weren't her sort of people, it was quite obvious. Their dear old stables to be given a makeover and filled with smart horses and smart people, their wonderful freedom to do what they liked to be snuffed out by Miss Snout-in-the-Trough …

'We can't let this happen!'

'We shall die!'

Joe looked sympathetic. 'I can guess how you feel. Like me.'

He thought they were going to cry so said, 'I'm sorry if I've spoilt your day. I'll leave you to it. Go and wait in the car. Thanks for the coffee.'

Millie and Imogen went back into Bluebell's box and stared at each other over his back.

'It can't be as bad as I think it is,' Imogen said.

'It is. A hundred pounds a week … '

'Jake had better dig up that treasure fast! We need it.'

'Before Snout-in-the Trough concretes it over.'

'Snout-in-the-Trough ?'

'My father said she was one of those – people with snouts in the trough.'

'It's a good name for her. Snouty.'

'Polly Power, she said.'

'Polly High and Mighty. It suits her.'

'She's awful.'

They went back to grooming Bluebell but Millie kept sniffing because she thought she was going to lose her new pony. They discussed keeping the ponies in Mr Hodge's cattle yard but Imogen said her parents would never let her cycle along that road to get to it and walking would take her too long (and kill her just the same) and Millie said it was horrid anyway, all mud and nowhere to keep their stuff and nowhere to ride either, except in the close-by fields.

They hung around, hoping to hear what Polly Power's meeting with Miss Brocklebank had decided, hoping that, after all, Miss Brocklebank had told her to take a running jump. But no such luck. When she came back, Joe got out of the car and they both came into the stables again and she started to talk excitedly what she was planning to do. Millie and Imogen stood listening without bothering to hide this time.

'The old girl said I could do what I liked, as long as I don't touch her garden. Well, that's not a problem, although it would be a good place for the arena – that'll have to go on the other side now, if we can find the flattest place. She gave me the name of the local builder but I think I'll get my London builder to do it. These locals, round here – they're in the dark ages. It'll take for ever.'

'You've got to get planning permission,' Joe said. 'The locals might be better at that, knowing everyone, like.'

'A bit of cash shoved the planners' way will help, surely?'

Imogen piped up, 'My uncle's in the planning department. He's a jobs-worth and if you try to bribe them he'll refuse you permission point blank, whatever you want.'

Polly glared at her. 'Did I ask your opinion?'

'I was helping you, so you don't make a big mistake.'

Millie, emboldened, said, 'It's in the flood plain too. The river floods quite often. I shouldn't think you'd get permission.'

Snouty smiled patronisingly. 'I've a lot of experience in these matters. I don't think you two should worry too much about my problems.'

'They're ours too,' said Imogen. 'If you're coming here.'

'Well, when I come, I don't expect you'll be here.'

With which she stalked out and drove smartly away.

'You shouldn't have put her back up,' Millie said. 'We've got to be smarmy and helpful so that she likes us. Then we stand more chance. And you haven't got an uncle in the planning department. If you have it's the first I've heard of it.'

'No. But my cousin Josh makes tea for the Environmental Health Officer and sometimes the planners ask him for biscuits.'

When they parted Millie decided she would have to come clean with her parents about Bluebell. Now Snouty had arrived their curiosity would be fully engaged and she could slip in about Bluebell as an extra and hope they would hardly notice. Miss Snouty Power was bound to take all their attention.

As it already had. They knew about her visit, with a young man, and that she had visited Miss Brocklebank. They didn't know how foul she was, and what she was planning: at least Millie was ahead on that.

'A whole new stable block and an arena.'

'Well, she won't get that. It's in a flood area.'

'She said she'd bribe them. No problem.'

Mike Hodge laughed. 'I'd like to see old Colonel Brigstock's face when she offers him a brown envelope! Poor girl. She's put her money on the wrong horse there. He's uncorruptible.'

'Incorruptible,' said his wife.

'One of the old school. Fine.'

'I don't see, if she really wants it, why she can't improve the interior without permission. She doesn't want change of use. It's always been stables. She's only got to put a new floor in, new partitions and things. What's the problem?'

'Well, I suppose she wants a swanky front. Impress the neighbours. She 'd do better to improve the cottage. It'll fall down any day now.'

'I can't see Miss Brocklebank living happily with a type like that, poor old dear. And how are you children going to get on with her, Millie – as you spend more time down there than in your own home? She won't want you lot underfoot.'

'Imogen's got her pony there. And the Creambuns. And there's a stray pony we've taken in. It was loose down by the river…'

The story came out. To her amazement her father laughed and said, 'Sitting tenants then. You've got rights, if Miss Brocklebank stands by you.'

'Do you think so?' This was a new idea to Millie.

'Stick up for yourselves. She sounds a right tyrant. Not our sort. I'll have a word with Miss Brocklebank.'

No mention of the new pony, paying for it, all the harrumphing Millie had expected. Her father on her side! Millie couldn't believe her ears.

Chapter 4

'Listen! I told you!'

Jake stood in the middle of Miss Brocklebank's vegetable garden with his metal detector thrust into her astounding bed of leeks. Millie and Imogen had to admit to being impressed by the manic chuntering of his darling machine.

'This is where it is. Under here.'

'What is? Granpa Brocklebank's old Ferguson tractor?'

'His false teeth?'

'Granma's tin bath?'

'You can't dig under there. She'd go bananas.'

'Not if she got half a million. The land owner gets half. You can scoff! I'm going to dig it up as soon as I get an opportunity. I can lay the leeks to one side and replant them when I've finished. She needn't ever know.'

'But she never goes anywhere long enough.'

She had departed now to fetch her old age pension, which took under the hour. Jake had watched her trundle away down the drive to catch the bus.

'At night time, perhaps. We'd have plenty of time then.'

The garden was on the flat river meadow that lay at the bottom of the hill on which the Hodge farm stood. The wall of the stable block sheltered the top half of it; at the bottom Miss Brocklebank's dilapidated cottage separated it from the river. Her kitchen door opened straight into the garden, and was nearly always open, as she went in and out all day. The kitchen floor, covered in terrible old lino, was as muddy as the flowerbeds themselves and the kitchen was nearly as full of flowers as the garden itself, standing in pots all over the table, sideboard and window sills: 'The delicate ones, dears. They need me.' The garden was a magnificent tangle of roses, clematis, lilac, daisies, lupins, delphiniums, lavender, dahlias, geraniums, red hot pokers and hundreds of nameless, prolific flowers, plenty of weeds ('wild flowers, dears, not weeds') and, at the top end, the incredible leeks, the gargantuan cabbages, the Brussels sprouts hard and round as golf balls, the onions like shiny brown cannon-balls, carrots a foot long, marrows like miniature submarines, lettuce and parsley and basil and tarragon running amok in every crevice and screens of runner beans like flowering curtains. She gave the children basketfuls of stuff to take home and carers came from the village once a week to collect the surplus. How much of it she ate herself was a mystery, for Miss Brocklebank was spare and bony, but Millie reckoned she must get her full five healthy veg a day at least. They kept their manure heap especially for her, outside the door that gave on to her garden (on top of the Roman treasure, as Imogen pointed out to Jake) alongside the leeks.

'As soon as I get the chance,' Jake said.

At least it seemed that Polly Power, having taken one peep into the cottage, declared that she would rent a flat in the village until she had 'done it up'. So far Miss Brocklebank had declared that she did not want it done up. Millie guessed that her stand would be broken down, unless the bony old frame possessed a steel not yet revealed. There was no planning permission forthcoming for the rebuild Polly wanted for the stable as Mike Hodge had foretold, but she had decided that she was going to modernise the interior, and her smart builders from London were already unloading their bricks, timber and concrete mixers in the yard.

'Get your ponies out. They're in the way,' she had told the girls.

'They live here,' Imogen said.

'In the field then. Those sort are better out than in.'

'It's spring and the grass is too rich. They'll get laminitis if they're out all the time.'

Snouty could not deny the truth of this. She was beginning to dislike Imogen intensely.

'Make room for them amongst the junk on the other side of the yard then, where I can't see them.'

So Millie and Imogen, with help from Jake and his sidekick Harry, a football freak (going to be goal-keeper for England by the time he was twenty) carried, pushed, pulled and dragged the paraphernalia of a hundred years' farming out into the yard and left it piled up in the way of the London builders. There were large double doors on this side of the yard, as this had once been the threshing barn, and out of it they hauled old chaff cutters, oat-crushers, parts of an elevator, half a tractor, a hay cart, gun-dog kennels, a pony trap without wheels, large tin feed-bins and piles of sacks, broken flower-pots, buckets, rotting hay bales, decomposed harness and sweepings of rat dirt. The debris took up more of the yard than the builders' materials and were very much in the way.

'We're helping you tidy up the place,' Imogen pointed out to the furious Snouty. 'You should pay us, really, for all the work we've done. It's taken hours and contractors would charge at least twenty pounds an hour.'

The contractors hired to remove the stuff shortly afterwards did indeed charge more than twenty pounds an hour, having picked up from the London gang that 'the missus is mega-rich. Lay it on, mates.'

'Round one to us,' Imogen crowed as they surveyed their new, magnificent domain. Now empty of all the rubbish, the barn was like a cathedral, and all theirs.

'The ponies can go up one end, put some bars across—'

'Paint goal posts on the end wall and it's big enough to practise penalties,' said Harry.

'No way,' said Imogen firmly. 'You can do that outside. You can have one corner and Millie and I'll have the other, for our stuff, our things.'

They started making it like home. Millie and Imogen filled the ponies' end with straw, deciding the two animals could live together, no partitions, and forced the boys to knock them up fencing across the width of the barn, with a slip rail for access. The floor was hard earth and they were able to hammer in posts after flooding it with the hose 'borrowed' from the builders. They also 'borrowed' a few planks for the fencing, taken from the dismantled partitions that had been stripped out of their old barn. The builders were quite friendly and in conversation Jake discovered that the first thing they were going to do, now the barn was stripped, was concrete the whole floor of Miss Snouty's new stable. That put Jake in a panic.

'Over my treasure!'

He decided he must have another dig there before the deed was done in case it was ages before he got a chance to attack the leeks. He decided to dig there again immediately the builders left for the day.

'No one will see me. Tell Mum and Dad I've gone to football with Harry. Then you can help me, if you like.'

'I don't like really,' Millie said. 'But I might.'

The strange thing was that no one had ever mentioned her ownership of Bluebell again, her parents having apparently forgotten all about it and Miss Brocklebank, although knowing the pony was there, never asking any payment for his rent. Millie fed him with the family hay which she carted on her bicycle from the farm so he wasn't costing Miss Brocklebank anything. Snouty had never mentioned him again, although both the girls guessed that the question of their place in the scheme of things would arise when the livery stable was properly under way. Imogen's idea was that they would have to make themselves indispensable to Miss Power so that she would have to put up with them, but how they were to do that she hadn't yet decided. The builders reckoned they would only take a week to revamp the interior of the stable and then the new horses were going to arrive, so there wasn't much time to work anything out.

'Play it by ear,' Imogen said. 'She won't get rid of us, whatever happens.'

Millie wished she felt as confident.

But she went down to find Jake in the stable after tea. He had coerced Harry into helping him and they were there already and after a bit Imogen turned up, because she wanted to be in on the treasure. That was four people who knew about it now, Millie thought. Not so good. It only needed Snouty to turn up …

It was a bit crowded with four of them scratting around in the corner so Millie left them and wandered down the familiar barn, scuffing her feet in the ancient grooves and dips in the brick floor worn by the great hooves of carthorses long since dead. To be obliterated in the morning: it seemed sad to think of this link with the past being wiped out. She supposed she ought to be glad for the place to look smart but she wasn't. She liked it as it was. She was a sad person.

Screams came from the corner where the digging was going on.

'Steady on!' Jake shouted. 'Leave it! Leave it!'

'It's huge —'

'No, it's in two pieces. Don't use the spade. Get out of the way!'

Millie hurried back. The hole was quite big and three behinds were sticking out like terriers' bottoms out of a rabbit hole.

'What is it?'

'Treasure!' shouted Imogen.

Jake shuffled backwards holding something in his hands. It looked to Millie like just a bar, like a bit of old door hinge. They all crowded round but Jake pushed them away, making for the window.

'I need to take it to the light.' He was trying to brush it clean with his handkerchief.

'What is it?'

'Get some water to wash the earth off.'

Imogen ran to fetch Barney's water bucket and Jake put the bar in, washing it with his handkerchief. It was not very big but with the earth cleaned off it showed an embossed pattern down its length with what looked like red stones set in the middle of the curves. It appeared to be of a metal like bronze or iron.

It was only a bit of something, but it certainly wasn't a bit of an old tractor.

They all stared at it, awestruck.

'Are they rubies?'

'It's real treasure! It's not rubbish.'

'It's a secret,' Jake said, very serious. 'Remember, not a word to anybody. Not parents or anybody.'

He was white with excitement, cradling the bar.

'Especially not Snouty.'

As if on cue, they heard a car door slam in the yard. It was just becoming dusk and Millie saw out of window Snouty and Joe getting out of the Porsche, parked up beyond the builders' paraphernalia. She squeaked a warning.

Jake, clutching the bar, made for the side door leading up to the farm and ran. Harry followed.

'We can't leave it like this!'Imogen hissed at Millie. 'Start filling it in! She might come and find something else.'

The two girls ran back to the corner and started frantically shovelling the loose earth back into the hole. It went easily but they were never going to move it all in the few minutes it took for Snouty to arrive. They heard her in the doorway.

'They're starting tomorrow and say it'll be finished within the week. I've planned for six loose-boxes down here. There's room for seven really, but I'd rather give the horses plenty of room. What do you think?'

'Looks okay to me' said Joe, without much interest.

'There's only four of us, for a start, but I'm sure I can find another two or three without much difficulty.'

'Who are the other two?'

'Amy and Alex.'

'Ugh,' said Joe.

After a pause, 'Where've the little girls gone? Have you got rid of them?'

'Not entirely, unfortunately. They're in the next barn for the time being. They'll have to go eventually. Those dreadful ponies can't be part of a decent stable.'

Imogen snorted. Millie hissed at her.

Polly said, 'The builders are starting to concrete the floor tomorrow. The two ends are still earth, can you believe?'

She moved forward to prove to Joe the pathetic state of the floor and found, beside a pile of earth, Millie and Imogen staring at her. Clearly startled, she snapped, 'What on earth are you doing here?'

'Er, digging,' Imogen admitted, there being no proof otherwise.

'Digging?'

'We heard the builders say they were going to concrete the floor over tomorrow and we know there's a dead horse under here and we wanted a few bones for our biology lesson. We found its jawbone a little while ago.'

'Really? That's a coincidence. Have you still got the jawbone?'

'It's around somewhere.'

'Because if you have, I'd really like to borrow it. I have to give a lecture on the horse's mouth at the Equestrian Centre and a real jawbone would be really useful. Could you lend it me?'

'Er, yes. Of course.'

'Great. I'll collect it sometime next week, if I may.'

'Umm.'

For once Imogen was lost for words. Miss Power then wandered off still nattering to the uninterested Joe, leaving Millie and Imogen staring at each other in horror.

'Well, you can say you've lost it,' Millie said.

'I thought it was in my underwear drawer but now I can't find it.'

'Perhaps you can get one from the knacker's. My dad's friendly with the knacker.'

'I can't go to the knacker's! I'd rather die.'

'He doesn't do humans.'

They started to get giggly again.

'A jawbone, a jawbone! My kingdom for a jawbone!'

'The butcher'll give you a jawbone.'

'Not equine. Do you think I can give her a cow jaw and she won't notice?'

'If she does notice we can say we thought it was a horse.'

Which is what they did, save the jawbone the butcher gave them did look very contemporary with bits of flesh stuck to it here and there and a very new stink. They scrubbed it clean and buried it outside in the grass to mature. How well did Snouty know her anatomy?

Rather well, as it turned out. She came in on Saturday morning while the girls were gawping at the astounding new stables that had gone up in the last few days on top of the immaculate concrete floor. The row of loose-boxes made their old barn look like the interior of a racing stable; they scarcely recognised it.

They produced the jawbone, now looking relatively ancient, and Polly took one look at it and said, 'That's a cow's jaw.'

'Oh really?' Imogen looked suitably wide-eyed. 'Are you sure? We thought it was horse.'

'Then you thought wrong.'

'Oh, we're sorry. Our mistake. We really did think it was horse.' She put on her most ingratiating smile and said, 'If you are very good at horses' mouths, could you take a look at Bluebell and tell us how old he is? We don't know, you see, and we want to know if he's old enough to ride.'

They led her into what they called now 'their' barn and the

40

two ponies in their enclosure came to the rails with their noses fluttering a greeting.

'Which is Bluebell?'

Millie got hold of Bluebell's forelock. 'This one.'

Polly stepped up and yanked the pony's mouth open, peered in, and said , 'Rising five.'

'Oh good.'

They were about to ask her how to tell, but she had lost interest in Bluebell and was now looking about her, taking in their comfortable quarters. The boys had imported an old sofa, and they had knocked up a table with an old door and two big oil cans and brought home two rickety chairs from the tip. Tea mugs (clean luckily) and a tin of biscuits stood on the table.

'Very nice,' said Polly thoughtfully. 'We could get another six boxes in here later.'

'But we're all right in here for now, aren't we?' Imogen appealed, looking pathetic. (No wonder she got the leading roles in the school's drama club, Millie thought as she watched her.) 'We're in here a lot, you know, and we could keep an eye on your horses when you're not here. You know what livery stables put in their advertising: twenty-four-hour supervision?'

'Except you're at school all day and in bed all night. Not much twenty-four-hour supervision there,' the woman said tartly.

'But I'm very close if something happens in the night,' Millie put in. 'Closer than you, until you move in with Miss Brocklebank.'

'Well, that's not going to happen in a hurry. There's no way I can live there until the cottage is rebuilt.'

The girls guessed that old Miss Brocklebank might be objecting to having her cottage rebuilt. People had been trying to persuade her for years to no avail. Perhaps Snouty had met her match in the stubborn old woman.

'When are the horses coming?'

'I'm bringing mine and Joe's next Saturday. Then two others will come later. For now.'

When she had gone the two girls considered their fate.

'I think,' said Imogen, 'we have to make ourselves indispensable to her. Somehow. So she lets us keep our ponies here for nothing. Suck up to her.'

'You mean muck out and that?'

'Well, none of them live nearby, do they? Even if we fed the horses in the morning and turned them out, that sort of thing. For our keep, your keep mainly, as my parents pay and yours don't.'

'So it's me that's got to feed them in the morning and turn them out?'

'Er, yes.'

'Thank you.'

'You want to keep Bluebell, don't you? It was me who found out how old he is. You ought to be full of gratitude.'

'Yeah. I ought.'

'At least you can ride him now.'

They forgot Miss Power for the time being, once they had found out Bluebell was rideable. Who knew whether he had ever been ridden before? They tacked him up with Barney's saddle and bridle, to which he had no objection, and led him out into the field. The two Dartmoors, Dodo and Duffer, came cantering up, goggle-eyed at the newcomer. Imogen shooed them away and held Bluebell's reins while Millie climbed gingerly into the saddle from off the fallen tree they always used as a mounting block. She sat down gently. Imogen held on, but all Bluebell did was yank his head down to try to graze.

'He doesn't mind. He must have been broken in once.'

Imogen led him forward and Bluebell went obediently. They walked round in circles and tried a trot and Bluebell behaved perfectly.

'We can go for a ride together! I'll get Barney.'

'We've only got one saddle and bridle.'

'You can use them. I'll ride bareback and use a headcollar and lead rein. Barney won't mind.'

They set off cautiously across the field towards the river. There was a ford where they always crossed and a raised footbridge for walkers, for the track was a public path, coming from the village. Across the river the path followed some way along the far bank. The land on this side of the river rose up a wooded hillside where the girls knew all the ways. On top of the hill was Standing Hall, which they kept clear of as they were aware they were trespassing, but no one ever came out and shouted at them. The house was old and was said to be inhabited by a loony old lady who never came out beyond the confines of her garden. An upmarket Miss Brocklebank, Imogen called her. The garden was very beautiful and was open to the public once a year, in aid of the local church. The girls had visited but had been more interested in the old stable yard behind the house, a more elegant and well-kept version of their own yard, where once the house's carriage horses had been kept, and the family's riding horses and hunters. Millie's father said that in the past the proprietor of Standing Hall had owned all the land including their own farmhouse and Miss Brocklebank's place.

'Ours and Miss Brocklebank's were just the farm that belonged to the house. They up there were the toffs, and us down here the workers. All changed now, of course. The old lady up there is the last of a line. When she goes it'll be bought by a city banker with his bonus, or a footballer.'

Millie related what her father had said as they rode up through the woods towards the old mansion.

Imogen said, 'How about Snouty, with her divorce settlement? It would suit her far better and Miss Brocklebank could grow her leeks up there–'

'And when she's gone Jake could dig up her garden and find his treasure. That would be great.'

'Except it won't happen, of course.'

'Pity.'

But the idea stayed in their minds: the thought of their own stable yard back and Miss Brocklebank spirited away.

'When Snouty's horses come, we'll have to hack up here with her so that she sees how much happier she would be with a place like Standing Hall.'

'Yes, she fancies herself Lady of the manor. She could make an offer, even if it's not for sale.'

It was lovely riding the two ponies together through the woods. In the past Millie had had to run behind, save when Imogen had sparingly given her a turn in the saddle, and she had only ridden Barney up here alone when Imogen had been away on holiday. But with the two together it opened up a whole new experience.

'We can go miles at the weekends, take a picnic,' said Imogen.

'But we need another saddle and bridle first. I bet my parents won't shell out.'

'I'll tell mine my saddle's worn out. It is, fairly. And they'll buy me a new one and you can have mine.'

Now Bluebell had proved himself so amenable, Millie 's worries returned about paying the livery bill. No one had asked her for any money so far. She doubted if this happy state of affairs would last long. Perhaps her father would pay, if she caught him in a good mood. If Snouty wanted to get rid of them, she would put up the rates and then he certainly wouldn't pay.

But it was stupid to worry when she was so happy with her ride. The woods were in the glorious mantle of early summer, full of birdsong, even out of earshot of the beastly road. The two ponies went amicably, winding their way along a peaty path that led round the back of the hall. Bluebell was too good to be true, walking up eagerly, moving smoothly into a trot when Imogen kicked Barney on ahead of him. No bucks or napping, no head-snatching, no spooking. Then Millie started to worry that he was such a good pony someone must be looking for him. Not that Snouty thought so – how rude she was! Why did she worry so? Imogen never worried about a thing. Even now she was riding boldly round the back wall of the stable yard, only a hundred yards from the house itself.

'I've never been up here before. It's great, isn't it?'

She pulled up and looked down towards the river. Now clear of the trees, there was a fine view of the river below, winding towards the village and the bridge under the busy road. The traffic whizzed along in both directions looking like toy vehicles but they were too far away to hear it. The house stood serenely facing the view, its access driveway curving away on the side furthest from them to enter the village on the far side.

'It's beautiful.'

Millie sat looking, thinking how marvellous it was to have a pony to ride with Imogen, just what she had always dreamed of.

If only Snouty hadn't arrived on the scene!

Chapter 5

'I don't know why you don't tell Mum and Dad about this,' Millie said to Jake.

She was in his bedroom examining the bits of loot that he had dug up from the stable floor. The latest bit, a short, flat bar with engraved leaves and flowers and red stones in the middle of the flowers, was bent and broken but obviously very old. She was as convinced as Jake now that he really had found treasure.

'It's mine,' he said fiercely. 'If I tell them – just think ... Dad will scoff, Mum will believe it and persuade him, they'll go to Miss Brocklebank to see about digging there and she'll go bananas, everyone will hear about it and, who knows, some crook will come in the night and take the lot. I want to dig it up myself. It's mine.'

Millie could see his point. She guessed that all the treasure in the world would mean nothing to Miss Brocklebank compared to her leek bed. Money meant nothing to her.

'One day she's bound to go away somewhere, give me a chance.'

'She never does,' Millie pointed out.

'No. Well, I don't mind waiting. She's terribly old. She'll fall down the stairs or something sooner or later. Die.'

'Don't be so horrible. More likely the house will fall in on her.'

'I'll wait. Your Miss Power might well get rid of her, if I'm lucky.'

'Blimey, we mustn't let her find out!'

'No way.'

'She's bringing her horses tomorrow. The first two, hers and the computer nerd's. I think she'll start making me pay rent for Bluebell and Dad'll go bonkers.'

'She can't charge you much, surely? Especially now they're out at grass.'

'I'm keeping my fingers crossed. Imogen says I've got to suck up to her, make her my friend.'

'Can't think she's got many. You could be a first.'

All the same, both Millie and Imogen were quite excited about the arrival of the new horses. They raced home from school to find an enormous shining horsebox parked in the yard and Snouty just climbing out of the driving seat.

'Oh, good,' she said, 'you can help me.'

She looked straight out of an advertisement in her country clothes, the sort London people wore to go to point-to-points and game fairs, not the sort working country people wore on their farms. The highlights in her blonde, artfully tousled hair twinkled in the late afternoon sunshine. She smiled a pearly white smile. Amazing!

Millie and Imogen gawped.

'I've got two of them in here, mine and Joe's. We'll take mine first. She's the boss.'

They could hear loud kicking from inside the lorry, presumably from the boss. Just like her owner, the girls decided. But Millie, remembering she had to make herself indispensable, ran forward to help let down the ramp. Snouty ran up and presently came down again leading 'the boss', a tall, liver-chestnut mare. She was undeniably beautiful. She stood looking about her, ears pricked, large intelligent eyes taking in the strange place. There was no white on her and her coat was dark, almost dark brown, but with the reddish cast that made her a chestnut, with her mane and tail the same colour.

'Wow,' said Imogen.

'She's beautiful, isn't she?' Snouty said, suddenly quite human and mumsy. Millie could see now why she was so derisive about poor Bluebell. 'She's gorgeous. What's her name?'

'Red Sky. But we call her Snappy.'

Millie, who had been thinking about offering to do early morning feeds, was not encouraged by this stable name.

'Is she? Snappy?'

'Yes. I'm afraid her stable manners are atrocious. But once on her back, then she's an angel.'

As Millie knew she was unlikely to discover the 'angel' attributes, she was not comforted.

'You can hold her while I get Joe's. Keep your hand up close, under her chin, and jerk it back if she tries to bite you. Stand away from her.'

Dear Bluebell, Millie breathed, gingerly taking the lead-rein. The mare immediately snapped out at her and she jumped back with a squeak but didn't let go, too frightened of Snouty to fail.

'Pig!' she shouted, and gave a quick jerk as instructed. It was called self-defence. She got the idea, standing well away with her arm stretched out, her hand stoutly on the lead-rein where it connected with the headcollar.

'I'll get the pitchfork,' Imogen whispered, and they started to get the giggles. 'She's just like her owner. Animals are, everyone says so. That's why Barney and Bluebell are so nice, like us.'

'What does a computer nerd's horse look like, I wonder?'

'Dull.'

Strangely Joe's horse was quite dull compared to Red Sky. The mare was all thoroughbred but Joe's horse was built like a tank, a dark bay with an amiable, slightly surprised expression on his kind face.

'What's his name?' Imogen asked.

'Renkum Agostini de Ness Twitterwake.'

'You're joking!'

'No. We call him Wake. He's a darling. Joe doesn't know how lucky he is.'

Snappy was to go in the end box where Dodo and Duffer had been, on top of Jake's treasure. Wake went next to her. The two girls had to admit they did add glamour to the old barn and couldn't help feeling quite excited to see the two aristocratic heads looking over the half doors.

'Are there any more coming?'

'Two more. The Equestrian Centre is annoyed at us leaving to come here, taking two of their other liveries with us. So we thought we'd better do it gradually.'

'Is that where you were before then? At Standing District Equestrian Centre?'

'Yeah. I knew Auntie lived nearby and saw the possibilities of this place, having it for myself.'

'And us,' said Imogen. 'We come with it.'

Snouty actually laughed.

'I'm working on it,' she said. 'Treat me to a cup of tea in

your barn – I'm dying for a drink. Then I might think more kindly of you.'

'We're no trouble,' said Imogen, 'When treated properly.'

'We might strike a bargain, agreed.'

The bargain, it transpired, was mucking out and giving the early morning feeds.

'That's you, Millie. You're so near,' said Imogen. 'The feeds, I mean.'

Millie was in the habit of visiting the ponies on the way to school so it would not be a lot of extra work. Except—

'What about Snappy, if she's so horrible? I don't want to get killed.'

'I'll put the feeds ready in mangers that hang over the door. You needn't go in. Not to Snappy anyway.'

Polly Power, lounging on the boys' sofa with her mug of dubious tea, was suddenly sounding quite human.

'The trouble here is having no arena. That's where we do most of our riding. We can make an arena in the field that will do for the summer, but come the winter when the ground gets soft it will be useless. I think I might have one built anyway and hope your dreadful planning people won't notice.'

'They're bound to see it from the road.'

'I thought we might put it behind the stable block, not so public, between the stables and the river.'

'It might get flooded there.'

'It might get built, that's the point. If it's concealed from the road.'

'There's good hacking on the other side of the river, across the ford.'

'We don't hack out very much.'

Poor horses, the girls thought, but didn't say.

'We turn them out in the daytime, while we're at work.'

At work? What work? They knew what Joe did but were too polite to ask what work she did, only relieved to know she wasn't going to be underfoot all the time. Amazed that she was turning out quite human. Smiling!

'I'll feed the horses now and leave them. But I'll come back in the car before I go to bed, see that they're settled.'

She parked the horsebox more out of the way in the yard, called up a taxi on her mobile and quite soon departed.

'Blimey, she's mellowed!' said Millie. 'Mucking out two boxes and putting the feeds over the doors is pretty good for free livery.'

'What about when the others come?' said Imogen. 'Amy and Alex? Mucking out four boxes, and our own, in the winter will take a bit of time.'

'Oh, that's ages yet. Amy and Alex might do their own.'

'I wonder what sort of horses they've got? Are they into dressARGE too?'

'I think we ought to take it up. Going round in circles and sideways – I bet Barney and Bluebell could do it.'

'We could get free lessons!'

'But do we want to, that's the point?' Millie recalled the lovely ride up through the woods to Standing Hall, just taking in the smell of the spring trees and listening to the birdsong. She thought dressage was probably very hard work. Not just sitting there, enjoying.

Snouty, when they saw her next, confirmed that it was.

'Snappy is not really made for dressage. People choose German or Dutch-bred horses on the whole, what are called sports horses; they aren't so volatile as thoroughbreds, steadier, more amenable. Wake is perfect for the job but Snappy isn't.'

'What about Barney and Bluebell?'

'They could try. They could do it, but they would always look a bit odd because of the way they're built.'

'What do you mean, a bit wonky?'

'Yes.'

'What's wrong with them?'

'Well, where shall I start? Head too big on neck too short,

shoulders too straight, back too long, too narrow through the front, pasterns too upright, feet too small, hocks too straight—'

'At least they don't bite,' Millie cut in.

'Teeth too blunt,' said Imogen.

'It doesn't mean they can't learn to do some dressage. Dressage is only obedience, in essence, and developing the horse's natural abilities.'

The two girls looked at each other. Did they want to develop their ponies' natural abilities? Maybe.

'Would you give us a lesson?'

'Fifty pounds an hour.'

They laughed.

'We'll get a book from the library,' Imogen said. 'You can learn things out of books for nothing. Are Amy and Alex dressage freaks as well?'

'No. And that's a bit annoying because I was hoping to persuade them to make a quadrille with Joe and me, to go in for competitions. In dressage, a quadrille is a foursome, usually to music. The Equestrian Centre wins all the competitions round here and I thought it would be nice to beat them. They think no one can beat them.'

'We could join you, to make a quadrille,' said Imogen obligingly. 'It would be original, wouldn't it, to have us in? A bit different. That's what everyone looks for, something different.'

Polly laughed. 'It would be funny.'

'Yes, that's what spectators want, a bit of fun. They get bored seeing everything so perfect. I went to a village dog agility competition a little while ago and it was nothing like the ones you see at Olympia on television: the dogs weren't very good and went the wrong way and under the jumps instead of over, and stopped to fight or have a pee and it was really, really funny. Everyone loved it.'

'If you were good up to the standard your ponies are capable of, it would still be quite funny, alongside me and Joe,' Polly said.

'If you want to win—'

'I left the Equestrian Centre because the woman that ran it was so obnoxious. I would love to beat her.'

The girls wondered how obnoxious she was compared with Polly but kept a tactful silence. Afterwards, comparing notes, they agreed that Polly was showing signs of being quite human.

'Okay, we'll try dressage,' said Imogen. 'I'll get a book. We can't afford fifty pounds.'

'You're so competitive,' Millie complained. 'Why can't we just ride about?'

'Yes, we can, but we can go sideways sometimes to try it out, and a little pirouette here and there.'

The next day she came with an ancient book under her arm. It was called *Equitation* written by a man called Henry Wynmalen, who appeared in the photos looking very old-fashioned in a soft sun hat and baggy jodhpurs.

'It's fantastic,' she said. 'Read it and you'll know everything. More than Snouty, I bet. Lots of diagrams about going sideways, and masses of photos of everyone doing everything beautifully.'

'Huh.'

Imogen could read massive books in a few days and actually remember everything in them. Unlike Millie. The next day she came with a book called *Classical Circus Equitation*.

'Look at this! It tells you how to teach a horse to bow. If we bowed at the end we would be sure to win! I bet Snappy can't bow.'

Millie looked and saw a photo of seven riders standing up on three horses, mostly on top of each other, and thought Imogen was being slightly optimistic.

'Where on earth do you find these books?'

'At the recycling depot. There's a bin for books. I get lots there. This has got lots about quadrilles.'

Millie flipped a few pages and paused at 'Teaching your horse to kiss'. There was a footnote that said 'Do not do this trick too often in case the horse takes to biting your face.' She was not impressed.

'Gives you something to work towards, doing a quadrille with Snouty and Joe,' Imogen said.

Millie didn't want something to work towards. GCSEs were bad enough. Perhaps Amy and Alex would be more her style. She realized they didn't know anything about this couple, even if they were adults or children. When Snouty came back they enquired.

'Oh yes, I was going to warn you. Alex's okay but Amy's a bit of a problem. In fact they gave her notice to leave at the other place, which is why I thought it would be quite a good time for me to leave too. And the others.'

Millie and Imogen exchanged glances.

'Problem? How a problem?'

Snouty sighed.

'You'll see.'

'You've got to give us a warning!'

She sighed again and seemed to wilt, as if life had suddenly got too much for her.

'I got involved, which was a mistake. Her family were neighbours and she was always a mischievous child but everything went wrong when her father walked out and her mother got a new bloke. A banker who thought he knew everything. Amy adored her father and after he left she went seriously wrong. She got excluded from every school in the county, ran wild. Banker-man thought buying her a pony, giving her something to love and getting rid of her all day in a livery stable might be a good idea, so he asked me to find her a suitable pony, which I did. But because it was his idea she decided she hates it. If her own father had bought the pony it would be a roaring success but because it was the idea of the man she hates so much, she just digs in her heels, hates the pony like she hates the man and makes everyone's life a misery.'

Millie and Imogen listened to this story with dismay.

'So now she's coming here?'

'Yes. '

54

'To make our life a misery?'

'Excuse me, this is my place now. I wasn't intending to take you on with it, remember. Amy Grimm is my customer and her father pays my bill. I choose my own clients. I'd rather not have Amy but I feel responsible.'

Miss Power was getting uppity again. They decided not to argue, knowing they hadn't very good grounds, but when she had departed they moaned together, dreading the arrival of Amy Grimm.

'What she said, about it being her place now and we've just got to lump it, is true. So there's nothing we can do.'

'We'll be Amy's friend and with our good guidance she'll turn into an angel and everyone will love her.'

'Even the pony?'

'Yes, the pony too. We'll love the pony, at least, even if we can't love Amy. Wait and see.'

Chapter 6

They didn't have long to wait. Amy and Alex arrived the next day, along with their horses in Polly's horsebox. Millie and Imogen saw a scowling square face rimmed with thick black wild hair staring at them through the window, and next to her in the middle seat an unbelievably gorgeous young man smiling happily, blonde hair as artfully tousled as Polly's, sky-blue rugby shirt matching his sky-blue eyes.

'Alex's a *man*!' Imogen breathed. 'Wow!'

What a surprise! They had expected a delicate mummy's girl somehow, or a boring, bossy, frumpy female with whom they would have no rapport, but this – the shock stunned them. They shrank back in the doorway of their barn to recover their composure.

'He's gorgeous!'

'Can't possibly be as good as he looks ...'

'He's helpful too – look ...'

He had jumped down from the cab and was already undoing the horsebox's ramp to pull it down. Polly was looking grateful and eager while Amy stood picking her nose, obviously not intending to do anything helpful. Polly went up the ramp and came down with the pony that was presumably Amy's, a very nice-looking, foursquare Welsh cob, bright chestnut with a flaxen mane and tail. Both Millie and Imogen were smitten with an instinctive yearning to own such a cracker, followed immediately by a guilt complex at betraying such disloyalty.

'Can't possibly be as good as he looks,' Imogen said again.

'Not sweet like ours.'

'No.'

All the same he had large kind eyes and made no protest when Amy took his halter and gave him a great jerk with the rope.

'Put him next to Wake. The box is all ready,' Polly said.

'Come on, pig,' said Amy.

Millie and Imogen were shocked.

She disappeared with the pony into the stable and the lovely Alex went up the ramp to fetch his horse. Millie and Imogen waited on tenterhooks to see what sort of animal the gorgeous man had chosen for himself.

'What do you bet?' Imogen whispered. 'An Arab?'

'Yeah. An Arab.'

They were right. Down the ramp pranced a beautiful snow-white mare with a perfect Arab head. She stood still and looked all round, just as Red Sky had done, as if waiting to be photographed. She was quite chunky for an Arab, fine but not at all feeble-looking. Even more desirable than the Welsh cob.

Millie and Imogen felt that the rating of Knoll Farm Livery Stable had suddenly been elevated to the top rank with the new intake, and sensed that crawling away into the undergrowth with their poor little ponies would be the decent thing to do. But bravely they emerged from the barn and Polly made introductions.

'Your mare is heavenly,' Imogen said to Alex, 'What's her name?'

'Sultan.'

'You can't call a mare Sultan! She should be Sultana.'

'Sultana? As, like, Stoneless Raisin or Glacé Cherry? She's Sultan.'

Alex was grinning. Imogen didn't quite know how to take him, only aware that she was stricken with love at first sight. The man, not the horse.

'Have you got ponies here?' he asked.

'Yes.'

'And what are their names?'

'Manky and Wonky.'

'Imogen!' Millie protested, shocked. 'They're Bluebell and Barney.'

'They just look manky and wonky.'

'Looks aren't everything,' Alex said kindly, obviously not believing a word he was saying.

He disappeared into the stable with his mare and Polly followed and the two girls retreated into their barn where Bluebell and Barney stood happily scratching each other's withers, unaware that they were now found seriously wanting.

Millie said, 'But we don't want to win any prizes, only ride about. You didn't have to say they were called Manky and Wonky.'

'I'd like to show them, all the same. That they're as good as they are, even if their heads are too big and feet are too small and all that rubbish.'

The trouble was, Millie thought with a sinking heart, that Imogen was by nature very competitive. Now the competition had arrived, she was finding Barney wanting. She hadn't noticed before, when no other horses had been around. Even with Bluebell arriving – well, Bluebell was no competition. But now …

'Well, I don't want to change anything. A week or two back I didn't have a pony at all, so I'm not complaining. And if you want to compete, you know your parents will buy you a better pony – you've only to ask.'

'I don't want another pony. I want to do it with Barney.'

'Do what?'

'Beat them.'

Millie thought Imogen was being uncharacteristically idiotic.

She was about to make another acerbic remark when Amy Grimm appeared in the doorway.

'Am I interrupting?'

'Yes,' said Imogen.

'I'm used to nobody wanting me. Doesn't bother me. Are these your ponies?'

'Yes.'

Amy came forward, not caring about her welcome, and leaned over the bar to look at Barney and Bluebell. They both stopped scratching each other and turned round and stepped towards her. Bluebell's nostrils fluttered a welcome. Millie had a sudden peculiar feeling that the girl possessed a natural rapport with the animals, the magic of the so-called horse-whisperer. But it couldn't be true, if she hated her own pony. She felt confused.

She said, 'Yours is a beauty. Your chestnut.'

'He's boring. I hate him,' said the girl. 'Boring, boring, boring.'

'Stodgy, you mean?'

'No. Just does everything perfectly. Wins everything. Everyone hates me because I win everything. A stuffed sack could sit on him and he'd do a clear round. So what's to like?'

Even Imogen couldn't think of an answer. It sounded heaven. She decided to change the subject, go on the attack.

'Polly said you were asked to leave the other place. Why was that?'

'Oh, I rode a few of the other horses sometimes. They didn't like it.'

'Without permission, you mean?'

'Yes. Quite often there was no one around. I tried them all, took them out, went for a gallop. It was great. And they loved it too, stuck all the week in their boxes. Too much food and no exercise. They galloped like crazy. I went at night-time quite often so no one would see me. But they found out in the end.'

Millie and Imogen were speechless with amazement. No wonder she got thrown out! She wasn't as horrid as they had been expecting: they were both full of admiration for her nerve. While they were still goggling, Jake and Harry arrived to work on the machine they were building in their corner of the barn. It was a sort of boat with wheels, amphibious, very ambitious and unlikely, in the girls' opinion, ever to work. After football it was Harry's great passion; he was the creator and Jake the scientific partner, trying to be optimistic. It took his mind off the frustration of not being able to dig for his treasure. He prayed every night for Miss Brocklebank to die but she remained as fit as a fiddle, gardening from dawn to dusk. Millie said it would rebound on him, praying for someone to die, and it would be he himself who would be stricken with a fatal disease, so he had changed his prayer to suggesting her house would fall to bits and she would have to move and take her gardening elsewhere. Millie thought this a far more likely occurrence. Polly had obviously given up on trying to make the old girl improve her cottage and was resigned to staying in her flat in Under Standing.

'Who's she?' said Jake rudely, noticing Amy. He was neurotic about not letting anyone else know about his find and thought four of them knowing was already three too many. Another one in their barn was obviously very dangerous.

'She's Amy,' said Imogen. 'She's got a pony here so she's going to be around. That's Jake,' she introduced, 'Millie's brother. This is Millie, that is Harry, Jake's friend. And I'm Imogen.'

They all stared at each other and the boys said 'Hi' suspiciously.

'They do their own thing,' Imogen added. 'They don't bother with us.'

As if to prove this fact the boys moved over to their side of the barn and started discussing whether it would be possible to use an old tractor engine to propel it or whether the engine would be too heavy once they got afloat and sink it.

Millie and Imogen were stuck with Amy, which seemed to be the start of a new adventure.

Chapter 7

Polly Power, having been refused planning permission for her arena, went ahead and built it anyway. She said no one could see it from the road as the traffic was so heavy a driver couldn't afford to glance sideways for even a minute.

She and Joe practised their dressage every evening but when they entered for the competition in the autumn they were beaten into second place by the duo from the Equestrian Centre. Polly was furious.

'The judges must be blind! Emma's horse wasn't even sound. And she had it in rollkur for ages beforehand, which is banned.'

'What's rollkur?' asked Millie.

Imogen said, 'You rein its head in so hard it can only see its back feet.'

'You're joking!'

Millie was worried that Imogen was still determined that Bluebell and Barney were going to compete in the big show next summer.

'That gives us masses of time to train them,'

'Train them to do what?'

'Something entertaining. It doesn't have to be strictly dressage, although that's what everyone does, but if you read the rules it says 'a competition to entertain the crowd by an exhibition of advanced riding'.'

'There's nothing very advanced about our riding.'

'No, well, we haven't advanced yet. We're going to start. We're at the beginning of advancing.'

'If I had the right horse,' said Amy, 'I would give them a spectacular display of advanced riding – jump into the crowd, jump
out again, ten times round the arena at flat gallop, jump over the
judges' table, through the tea-tent – it'd be great. Perhaps we
could work together on something.'

'And get Alex in. He could think up something. After all, he's
an actor.'

Alex had shown his mare in hand, which entailed dressing in
a shirt, tight waistcoat, a pair of pale trousers and a bowler hat
and running very fast beside his gorgeous mare as she floated
across the ring at an extended trot. The rapturous applause from
the spectators was as much for Alex as for the mare, it was quite
clear, and both Millie and Imogen were deeply impressed.

Amy was scornful. 'He loves dressing up. He only keeps
Sultan to show off.'

Alex himself agreed. 'But, of course, I love it! I'm sure I'm a
prettier sight than the fat ladies in tight jodhpurs wheezing up
and down. If you find a part for me in your whatever-it-is you
are going to do I will be only too pleased to participate.
Something heroic, of course, nothing silly.'

'So you can show off,' said Amy.

'Exactly. In a nutshell.'

'Well, I can't be heroic on my stodge of a pony,' said Amy.
'What can I do?'

'Sell it,' said Imogen. 'Swap it for something wild. The sort
you like.'

Amy looked stunned, silenced.

Afterwards Millie said to Imogen, 'You shouldn't have said
that. She might.'

'I was only joking. She asked, after all.'

'We're supposed to be a good influence on her, not encourage
her to do crazy things.'

They had been out riding together several times with Amy
and both had been impressed with her ease in the saddle. She

was a far better rider than either of them. Her pony was extremely well schooled, but the girls thought perhaps that if Amy rode either of their ponies, the ponies too might come together and look quite different, as if they knew what they were doing. Sometimes they watched Polly and Joe riding in the arena and they decided that Amy was a better rider even than Polly. Polly let her ride Red Sky one evening and the mare looked fantastic in her hands and did all the clever stuff just as well with Amy as she did with Polly.

Polly said to her, 'You're a natural. Why don't you let me give you lessons?'

'I don't need them.'

'That's the wrong attitude. If you're good without lessons, think how much better you could be if you worked at it under instruction.'

'Why?'

'Why anything, Amy? Why? Why do we bother? It's hard work and I often ask myself why I do it. And then I think, when it comes right after I've put all the hard work in, how rewarding it is, how fantastic when something really difficult comes off perfectly. And there's no why about it. It is just wonderful, the reward.'

The girls weren't used to Polly waxing lyrical and stood gaping at her. She was always so brisk and carping they mostly kept out of her way. She certainly had a work ethic; they had learned that her day job was running a fashion boutique in the county town. That was a full-time job and the horses were another so it was no wonder she was generally cross. Just like my father, thought Millie sadly, used to cross people around her. He had been harassing his MP about getting lights put in to stop the traffic at the bottom of their drive so that he could get his tractor and trailer across, but to little avail, and was now talking about selling up altogether and finding a new farm. Jake and Millie felt the cloud of uncertainty hanging heavily, and Jake was getting more and more neurotic about his treasure. Millie could not imagine life without Imogen and their life in the barn, messing about with the ponies and mocking the boys' lunatic efforts to make their amphibious car. Having Bluebell gave the messing about more purpose and she loved the hours she spent grooming him and schooling in Polly's arena with Imogen when the others weren't there. The dressage lark was quite catching and they schooled according to the instructions of Mr Henry Wynmalen in Imogen's dog-eared book – free! as Imogen pointed out. It was mostly riding according to Mr Wynmalen's diagrams: in circles, changing directions, stopping and starting and standing still. After a bit they went off for a ride, over the ford and up the hill into the woods. When they invited Amy to come with them she said, 'Boring! Boring!' and they were relieved. Her scornful presence was always discomforting.

'She's a pain. I wish she wasn't around,' Imogen said.

They stood in the ford on the way home, letting the ponies drink, swatting off the midges that swarmed in the late evening sunshine. This boring thing was what they liked best, watching the swirl of the current round the ponies' legs, smelling pony sweat and mown grass, the scent of meadowsweet, sniffing the first dank breath of evening on the water. The river was full, even after a hot summer, and Polly's precious arena, wedged between the water and the back wall of the stable, looked highly vulnerable to the two girls who had seen the river in spate in the winter.

'She's crazy putting it there. All the surface will wash away if it floods.'

The back of Miss Brocklebank's cottage overlooked the river. It had a bed of nettles on the bank, growing up to her back door that was never opened. It looked even worse from the back than it did from the front, the windows darkly curtained, the roof sagging, a jackdaw's nest crowning the precarious chimney. At least the front had the glorious garden to distract the eye from the cottage's lamentable state.

'Jake willing her to die makes me feel bad,' said Millie.

'She's the sort that doesn't, for ages.'

'No. But the thought of that stuff … maybe it's nothing, but somehow I think it is. Big, I mean. Jake is convinced. It's driving him nuts.'

'He's fairly nuts anyway.'

They nudged the ponies on, out of the river and round the side of the stockyard to take them in. Later they would turn them out to join Amy's sweet chestnut, which seemed to get very little work from his owner. The Greenbaum ponies had been taken away and were no longer to be seen in the field, having done as little work as Amy's Welsh cob Goldie the last year. Tummy and Bummy were now said to be concentrating on ballet.

As they arrived at the yard entrance Amy came prancing out on Red Sky.

'Hey, what are you doing?'

'What does it look like?'She held the mare in firmly, for the change of routine had excited Red Sky. She was charged up, powered by the adrenalin flowing through her rider. Imogen called riders like Amy 'electric bottoms'. Anything they rode came to life. 'If you sit like a suet pudding,' Imogen said, 'the horse goes all dozy. If your horse feels like bolting, think suet pudding.' But Millie had never sat on a horse that felt like bolting and did not envy Amy now. She was aghast on Polly's account.

'You mustn't! Polly will kill you!'

'She won't see, stupid.'

'It's not fair, Amy,' Imogen shouted, but Amy had let Red Sky go and was already out of earshot. .

The two girls sat watching, shocked. Polly never galloped Red Sky. Her fastest pace on the mare was a collected canter. But now the mare went like the true thoroughbred she was, her polished training thrown to the winds as she took the bit between her teeth and tore across the water meadows. She looked fantastic. The chestnut cob threw up his head and charged after her, kicking out behind with enormous bucks. Even Barney and Bluebell were infected by the excitement and started churning round in the gateway while their riders sat staring in horror.

'Polly would have a fit!'

But then admiration and envy triumphed in the girls' heads over indignation on Polly's behalf. They started to laugh, thrilled by the beauty of the flying mare. If only they had the same courage as the wild girl Amy! What must it feel like? Their ponies' fastest pace barely raised the dust.

'Wow, I wish that was me!' Imogen said.

'You wouldn't dare.'

'No, I wouldn't.'

By the time the mare had settled after several circuits of the meadows, Amy cantered back and shouted, 'Great, isn't she? I'm going for a ride.' With which she went past, splashed through the ford, and disappeared up into the woods at a spanking trot. Millie was just in time to shut the gate on the other ponies which were only too anxious to follow.

'She's crazy! Polly'll go mad.'

'She won't know, will she? Unless we tell her. And we're not that sneaky.'

'No, we won't. But it's wrong. It's not fair on Polly.'

They untacked their ponies, rubbed them down and turned them out for the night with the others. The first excitement over, they were now anxious for Red Sky's safe return, worried about the repercussions.

'Even if we don't tell Polly, which we won't, I bet she knows the next time she rides her that something has happened.'

'If Amy comes back, that is.'

They waited. They rang their parents to say they would be late, but as dusk closed in they became more and more anxious. If Amy had come off, the mare could be anywhere. They would have to ring Polly then. But eventually they heard the clatter of hooves in the yard and there was Amy dismounting, sliding down from a sweat-covered, mud-splattered, manic mare which, exhausted as it

67

was, found it impossible to stand still.

'You can't put her back in the stable like that!'

Even Amy had the sense to agree. She was as exhausted as the mare, but lit by a glee the girls had never seen before. Not the grumpy, rude, disagreeable Amy, but an excited, happy, exuberant friend, trying to tell them how marvellous it had been. Having waited, worried for so long, and now smitten with envy, they did not take to this new Amy kindly, but told her severely to walk the mare around until the sweat dried and try to get her settled. She would need a thorough grooming if Polly was to be deceived, and they didn't feel like helping Amy with that, given the mare's vicious habits in the stable.

They left her with the job, feeling mean, which made them both cross. Their evening had been lovely until Amy had appeared on Red Sky.

'She needs a challenge. A bad pony, as crazy as she is.'

'No one will care if she kills herself.'

That was the worst of it. No one was bothering where Amy was now. They both went home feeling disturbed and unhappy with their thoughts.

Millie's mother insisted on knowing what she had been up to, and Millie told her what had happened, very reluctantly.

'Don't tell Polly. Please. If she knows how her mare was treated—'

'It's not the horse I'm thinking of. It's the poor child. No one cares what she gets up to as long as she's out of the house. It's something that she's got you two for friends.'

'She's not our friend. We hate her. She's horrid.'

'Well, just count yourselves lucky …'

There was no answer to it. But Millie had a sneaking admiration for Amy and remembered how her face had been alight with a joy never seen before. It showed she was capable of something more than her usual grudging denigration of everything that came her way.

Chapter 8

Amy, fired up by her experience, remembered a thrown-away phrase of Imogen's, something about selling her pony and buying something that suited her better. She knew she was being unfair to Goldie her perfect pony, but she hated his perfection: he gave her no challenge. Not like Red Sky – that ride had been brilliant! Just thinking about it stirred her blood: being on the edge of catastrophe, barely in control, feeling the mare's wild heart beating in tune with her own. If she had an animal like that …

Well, no one would buy her a thoroughbred even if she sold Goldie for a good price. And perhaps anyway not all thoroughbreds were tearaways. She just wanted a challenge, something perhaps that nobody else could cope with. And a picture came into her head, remembering her sour days at the Equestrian Centre: a black gelding shut away in a distant box, the noise of his hooves banging on the door, Emma swearing at him … his owner paid her bills but never came near nor by. She couldn't ride him and nor could anyone else.

Amy's eyes started to gleam. What a brilliant idea! The horse was called Dragon, she remembered. Surely there was a deal to be done there? Unless the horse had gone by now? The idea filled her with excitement. No one could say Dragon was boring. That was the sort of horse she wanted.

She decided to go and find out if he was still there. It was some time since she had been back but she knew the routine would be much the same. Most of the horses had been ridden and put away for the night by ten o'clock and Emma went to bed shortly after. Amy knew how to get in round the back where there was no security and decided to go when with luck the place would be deserted. Her mother could be fobbed off with any excuse – 'Staying late at Rachel's' or something similar. She had fallen out with Rachel months ago but her mother didn't know that. Her mother didn't care anyway, obsessed with keeping her new boyfriend happy. Amy mooched around the village for an hour or two, throwing stones into the river from the bridge and buying chips, kicking a Coke tin down the high street and mucking about with a few stupid boys outside the pub, then sneaking off to the Equestrian Centre when it got dark.

It was, unlike Miss Brocklebank's, an imposing stable yard set amongst beautifully fenced paddocks, its impressive floodlit arena flanking the drive. Emma's bungalow was set apart, luckily, in a copse of trees, and there was no sign of her awful yapping terriers which meant she was off the territory. All was peace and quiet. A light was on in the tack room and two girls were drinking coffee in there but they did not see her as she walked through the yard. A few heads were looking out over the bottom doors and one horse whickered softly, but mostly the occupants were munching their hay and dozing. Behind the main yard was a smaller much less impressive yard for ponies and children where Dragon used to be. Was he still there? He had had a notice with his name on beside the door and a chalked addition 'Danger. Keep Off.' Amy thought, no worse than Red Sky, who had bitten her twice, painfully, the night she had tried to clean her down after her magnificent ride.

She had brought a torch with her and now shone it on the stable. Yes, the notice was still there. She went to the open top door and shone the torch inside. Dragon was not vicious like Red Sky, only very nervous and unpredictable, and she did not expect to be attacked. She heard him give a snort of surprise and saw him swing round from his manger. His eyes in the torch's beam gleamed red like a cat's eyes in a car's headlights and he stood staring at her with his head up as if prepared for flight, looking every bit as challenging as she remembered.

Oh, but he was gorgeous! Her heart gave a great bound. Of course he was the horse for her! He was, she knew, a Friesian cross; Friesians being the black horses used for pulling hearses. But not for him the sedate pulling of a hearse; the body would be flung to the four winds if he was asked to do such a job! He stood about fifteen hands, bigger than Goldie (perhaps she could say she had outgrown Goldie and needed something bigger?), and was rather leggy, with a high head carriage and a long flowing mane. He had no white on him, and had long ears and large, wild eyes, just as she remembered. His black coat gleamed in the torchlight. Was he still neglected, Amy wondered. He didn't look it. Perhaps someone else had bought him? The two girls in the tack room might know.

She switched off the torch and hurried back. The horse let out a deafening neigh after her, loud enough to bring Emma out of bed if she was unlucky, but Amy took it as an omen: he wanted her! The light was still on. Amy went in and the two girls started round in surprise.

'Hey, what are you doing in here?'

One of them knew her, and was none too friendly.

'Just visiting.'

'You'd better not let Emma find you here.'

'I don't want to see Emma. I just want to get in touch with the person who owns Dragon. I want to buy him.'

'You must be mad!'

'Do you know where she lives?'

'She's never around. She's not do-it-yourself. He's full livery. Emma just puts him out in the field sometimes so he doesn't kick his stable down. Everyone hates him.'

'Well, I'd do a straight swap with Goldie, if I can find her.'

'Goldie's worth tons more than Dragon. You must be daft!

But his owner's in the book, if you look.'

Of course! She had forgotten. There was a book in the tack room with all the owners' addresses and telephone numbers in case of emergencies. They were filed alphabetically under the horse's name, so she found it quite quickly under Dragon. The owner was local. Amy tapped in the number on her mobile.

'You're ringing her now? She's probably in bed and asleep.'

Time meant nothing to Amy.

'She'll think someone's died.'

Certainly the voice that answered sounded anxious. 'Yes, who is it?'

'I'm Amy Grimm and I want to buy your horse Dragon. How much do you want for him?'

'Er – what? Who?'

It took the woman some time to come to her senses, and then she obviously found the offer unbelievable.

'Are you joking or something? You want to buy him?'

'Yes.'

'I've been trying to get rid of him for years and no one will have him.'

'Well, I will. At least, I'll give you my pony Goldie in exchange and he's worth a lot of money.'

'But I don't want another horse.'

'But he's instead of money.'

'I'll have to ask Emma.'

'No. Don't ask Emma!'

Amy could see that it was going to be more difficult that she had foreseen.

Emma would contact her parents and once the adults were in there wasn't a hope of her getting hold of the likes of Dragon. Although it seemed to her that none of them cared if she lived or died, when it came to the point she knew they would try to look after her.

'Can I come and see you and talk about it?'

'Yes, that would be best, I suppose.'

'Now?'

'What, now? I'm in bed.'

'Do you want to sell him or not?'

'Yes, I'm desperate to sell him. He's costing me a fortune.'

'I'll come now then.'

She rang off. The woman's address was not very far off, in fact quite close to where she lived. The two girls were laughing their heads off.

'Some way to do a deal! You're crazy.'

'Don't tell Emma.'

She realized she had been really stupid to let these girls know what she was intending to do. They were bound to tell Emma in the morning. The gossip round the yard was always flagrant and everyone would know about her idiotic deal in no time.

It was no good telling them to keep quiet about it. To put them off she pretended she had changed her mind.

'I suppose it is a bit stupid. I'll go home and sleep on it.'

What a slip up, she thought as she left the yard. She was tempted to take Dragon there and then and gallop away, but common sense – as much as she possessed, which was very little – prevailed. Her mobile said it was ten past eleven. She hurried to the address she had memorised, a boring modern semi much the same as the one she lived in with her mother, and rang the bell. It was opened by a nervous looking woman in a dressing-gown, sort of twentyish Amy guessed, or even thirtyish, for she had worry lines on her forehead and frumpy hair.

'Oh, but you're a child!' she exclaimed.

'Yes, but I have my parents' permission to buy Dragon, if you'll sell him,' Amy lied. 'They have offered you Goldie in exchange.'

'I don't want another horse though.'

'No, but if you take Goldie, Emma will sell him for you for lots of money. How much do you want for Dragon?'

'Well, I asked for five hundred but still no one would have him.'

'Then you would make an enormous profit, if we do a straight swap.'

This seemed to cheer her up, smoothing out a few of her worry lines.

'Perhaps you had better come in.'

'It's rather late. You've only to say yes or no.'

'It seems very – sort of, er, odd—'

'But you do want to get rid of him? I'll take him. It's simple.'

'I ought to deal with your parents, surely?'

'No. They don't care about it. Do what you like, they said.'

'Well …'

Amy could see she was winning. She felt herself beginning to tremble with excitement at the prospect before her. Take Dragon now, in the night, and the deed would be done.

'Can I have his saddle and bridle?' Goldie's saddle would never fit him.

'Yes, the tack is here in the house.'

Fantastic! Having bludgeoned the poor woman into agreement Amy left the house before she could have second thoughts. The saddle was heavy but felt light as thistledown to Amy as she ran back down the road towards the Equestrian Centre. Surely the two in the tack room would be gone by now?

Yes. Now to try to take Dragon silently. To be caught would be disaster. She knew the way out of the back, away from the intruder lights. The back field let out on to a bridleway which skirted the back of the village and went up the hill to the big house that looked down on the river and Miss Brocklebank's. Very convenient. She opened the gate, ready, then went back across the field into the yard where Dragon's head could be seen, dark against dark, looking out over his door. Everything was quiet, not a sound.

She went up and talked softly to the horse, stroking his neck.

He was kind enough, licking her hand, lipping at the buttons on her jacket. She hoisted the saddle on the half door and gently drew back the bolt. Dragon backed away and she went with him, still talking softly, slipping the bridle reins over his neck. If he hadn't been ridden for so long she was afraid tacking up would be difficult, but he accepted the bit in his mouth without demur. It was a simple snaffle, not even a noseband, so there was only the throatlash to buckle and no problem. She lifted up the saddle and slid it as gently as possible on to his back, talking to him all the time. Quiet as he was, she could feel the tension in him, feel the trembling of his withers. She fastened the girth, but only loosely, knowing that a lot of horses objected to the first tightening, and then stood talking softly to him for some time, stroking his neck, scratching behind his ear. He liked it, she could tell. So far she had been lucky beyond belief. If only her luck was going to hold … The repercussions later would be terrible: she already knew that. But with the deed done, hopefully, they would have a job to undo it. Don't think of Polly, she told herself. The two daft girls, Millie and Imogen, might stick up for her. But Amy had never counted on friends, seeing as she had had very few.

'I'm going to have you, Dragon, my friend. You haven't got any friends. We must stick together.'

She led him out of his box and he came quietly. She took him through the gate and into the field where, feeling the grass beneath his feet and finding freedom at last from his claustrophobic stable, he started to dance and jiggle and pull hard against her hands. She wanted to mount, but couldn't. Her luck was running out.

He was so strong! She had great difficulty holding him, pulled half across the field by the reins. She knew if she let go, she would lose everything. If only she could get on his back! The struggle seemed to last for ever. She was pulled off her feet and dragged, stumbled upright, wrapped the reins tight round her hands and was dragged again to the end of the field. Breathless,

sobbing with frustration, she tried to manouevre him towards
the gate, but he would only run backwards. He hit the fence rails
with a crack and came to a standstill, and in that moment Amy
flung the reins over his head and made a desperate leap for the
saddle. She got one leg half over and the animal was off, Amy
hanging down his side with her arms round his neck and one
ankle frantically holding its grip over the cantle. She thought it
was all over with her, but the horse's long mane saved her from
destruction, as one hand caught a handful at its roots and enabled her to pull herself more over the saddle. It was touch and
go, as he was tearing round the field at a flat gallop, but at least
the movement was smooth and he didn't jink which surely would
have done for her. She wriggled and gasped her way into the seat
of the saddle until she was properly astride, then groped for the
reins. Once in position her confidence flooded back, the panics
overcome by a glorious feeling of triumph. The gallop was her
favourite pace and the fact that she couldn't stop it even if she
wished didn't trouble her. The field was large and empty and she
saw no danger, guessed how the horse felt to be out of his stable
at last. All she had to do was steer until he ran out of steam.

His head was down, his great mane flicking her face as she crouched low, loving every minute. Yes, this was the horse for her! She knew it! Her fabulous luck in tricking everyone to get what she wanted filled her with triumph and she laughed out loud as Dragon's hooves scorched the dark field. It was gone midnight now and they had the world to themselves, a half moon lighting their path, the thud of hooves the only sound. She was out on her own, her rare, favourite place in life, away from the strictures that came her way, the brow-beating, the anger that seemed to follow her like a black cloud. She and Dragon were a pair, unwanted, rejected, despaired of, but their spirit was unbowed. Dragon was proving it to her, his own spirit boosting Amy's and chasing away the dire thoughts she might be harbouring about what lay ahead for her in the immediate future, facing the enemy: Emma, Polly, her mother, the education department, the social service harridan, the do-gooders – oh! all the people who wanted to improve her! School her, get her to bow to convention, do the right thing. But all that was blown away by Dragon's gallop. If this was bolting – which it was – she loved it, she wanted it to go on forever.

But Dragon was unfit and soon he started to slow down and Amy came back to her senses, the euphoria fading. She took a pull and turned him for the open gate that gave on to the bridleway. Her eyes were used to the dark now and she knew this way. It was well trodden from the riding school. Dragon was obedient, but spooky and het up, snatching at the bit and dancing about. It felt like sitting on something likely to explode at any minute. In spite of the gallop he still wanted to go, but Amy was afraid now of losing him in the dark if she came off, and for once preferred a more staid pace, better safe than sorry. No wonder, she thought, as he pulled and shied and let fly the odd buck, that no one would buy him … There was no relaxing. She released him into a long-striding trot but that came with several large bucks and an ominous pulling on the bit that suggesting he was ready to gallop again. Amy, good rider as she was, was inexperienced with rogue horses but instinct told her to keep him calm and insisted on walk again. But it was a knife edge with Dragon, dicing with danger, nothing like the gorgeous, silky fire of the thoroughbred Red Sky, obedient to a fingertip. Any hesitant doubts that she might have bitten off more than she could chew Amy put firmly away. She had no choice: it had to work, her and Dragon. And she was starting now, riding him home with a mix of guile and persuasion, firmly fighting down any pricks of fear.

But she survived, riding round the big house on the top of the hill and looking down towards the river and the stable yard she now thought of as home. The headlights of one or two cars flickered along the road, but there was no sign of light in Miss Brocklebank's cottage nor in the Hodges' house on the hill opposite. She rode carefully down through the trees to the ford but here Dragon refused to cross. He whirled about and thrashed the edge of the water with a forefoot but refused to go in until Amy despaired. Closing her legs, facing him forward, she could get no advance. Eventually she slipped off and plunged in herself and to her great relief he relented and came with her. The water was icy, running fast, and came nearly up to her waist, but at least she was home, if frozen and exhausted.

It was lucky the stable yard was isolated for as she came in the horses in their boxes all let out excited whinnies, Red Sky and Wake, Sultan and Goldie. Luckily she had put Goldie in that evening instead of leaving him out in the field, so now she let him out of his box and led Dragon in instead. She untacked Dragon and shut the door on him, then caught Goldie who was nosing over the door at Red Sky and fetched his saddle and bridle. The prospect of riding him back to Emma's did not appeal, but it had to be done. She was now exhausted, limp from the shock of what she had achieved, and wanted only to crash out into unconsciousness. But if she didn't take Goldie back now all her good work would be undone.

As it happened, riding Goldie back to Emma's through the dark, silent woods and over the hill where a bright moon lit their path was balm to her jangled nerves. She was moved to wonder why she wasn't happy with such a paragon as Goldie, so sweet and obedient. But then the memory of her wild gallop on Dragon and that amazing feeling of fear and exhilaration mixed that had fired her miserable brain came back to her and made her laugh out loud. That was what she wanted! She put Goldie back into Dragon's box, filled his water bucket and haynet, kissed him on the nose and went home.

Chapter 9

When Millie went into the stable to dish out the feeds in the morning she got the shock of her life to find an excitable black horse in the box where Goldie had been the night before. She went to look for Goldie in the field but there was no sign of him. Polly hadn't said anything about a new horse coming, but Millie supposed that that was what had happened. She fed the horse and decided to ring Polly to say that Goldie had gone missing. Even then, at the back of her mind, she suspected Amy was to do with it.

All hell was let loose when the story was unravelled. Millie and Imogen kept their heads down, secretly full of admiration for Amy's daring. Emma and Polly both went bananas and blamed each other bitterly for the impasse, Polly more forcefully than Emma because she had got by far the worst side of the bargain. Amy's mother gave her such a pasting that Amy left home and came to live in the barn with Bluebell and Barney, at which Millie's mother rang the social services and Amy was removed. Whatever happened next no one really found out, but it ended up with Amy returning home, her mother placated, and Amy given permission to spend all her time, apart from her sketchy private lessons, with Dragon. A child psychiatrist said befriending the horse she so ardently desired and had gone to such lengths to acquire might do her the world of good, as nothing else they had tried with her had been successful. It never occurred to him that Dragon's part in the scheme of things might be questionable. Also Polly's bitter, 'Just gets her way in everything … Who's going to pick up the pieces? Me, of course', overheard by Millie and Imogen, prompted them to remind her that it was she herself who had brought Amy to their hitherto peaceful stable. 'Fool that I was!' was Polly's answer to that.

All the same, amazing opportunities opened up.

'This lark next summer, where we enter the competition to beat everybody, Emma especially, not to mention Polly and Joe – I've got all the time in the world to work on it now,' Amy said. 'Something really good. Me on Dragon, you on Barney and Bluebell, and perhaps Alex if he wants with Sultan because he's a natural show-off and he's got nothing else to do, after all.'

'Why, hasn't he got a job?'

'Well, he works with Polly in the shop. He's good there because he's so handsome and charming, all the customers love him. But he takes a lot of time off and Polly gets wild, but she can't really do anything about it because he lives with his doting mother and doesn't need the money. His mother's loaded and gives him everything he wants.'

'Blimey.'

Imogen and Millie considered the ways of the world, and the luck that fell the way of the undeserving. They had reconsidered their attitude to Amy since she had pulled off her amazing stunt and now gave her grudging admiration. It didn't mean to say that they actually liked her, as she was still rude and horrible, but her attitude to her new horse impressed them. He was as horrible in their eyes as his owner but they had to admit that her handling of his foibles was very clever. Imogen said she was a 'horse-whisperer', one of those rare people who had a special affinity with the horse, a sort of magic. Even Polly, who pooh-poohed such fancies, admitted that Amy was a bit special, horsewise. She had never had a lesson in her life but rode with a rare and natural grace. She was given dire instructions to ride only in the arena with the gate shut, but Millie and Imogen guessed – or knew – that she took Dragon out for a gallop when the rest of them had gone home. Where did she go? Around the whole neighbourhood they guessed, far into the night. It hadn't taken her long to teach him to cross the ford.

The ford was getting higher by the week and started to lap into Polly's precious arena. Millie and Imogen were trying not to say, 'We told you so,' but Polly knew they were thinking it. She swore roundly and started to box Red Sky and Wake over to a drier arena belonging to a friend the other side of the village for their sessions. Miss Brocklebank's cottage was looking vulnerable, as usual, and the do-gooders came, as usual, to try to persuade her to leave but she, as usual, declined.

Jake and Harry in the barn suggested that their amphibious vehicle might soon come into its own.

'I really don't see how it works,' Imogen said scathingly, surveying the decidedly odd machine that took up all the boys' side of the barn.

'It's more boat than car,' Harry admitted. 'The two things don't mix very well. We've got an outboard on the back for being on the water – that's okay, but fixing the engine out of my dad's old Robin Reliant for the car bit is a pig. Its weight sinks the thing so we need more buoyancy underneath, but then the wheels are in the way.' His voice petered out sadly.

'When the stable floods, it'll probably decide it's a car and sink,' Imogen said.

'No it won't. It will be a useful boat. We can ferry the horses to dry land.'

'They'll be safer swimming.'

'I hope it does flood – properly, I mean – so Miss Brocklebank has to get rehomed. Then we can dig,' Jake said.

Amy was in the other stable talking to Dragon as she usually did in the evenings, so the great secret could be discussed. It was never far from Jake's mind.

'The forecast for rain before Christmas is very bad – or good, if you look at it from your point of view,' Imogen said . 'Polly's beautiful stables are going to go under like they did before. We shall have to tell her because she didn't believe it when we warned her at the beginning.'

'Yeah, well, the horses won't drown. Only get their feet wet.'

'They won't like it.'

Since the stables had been rebuilt the foursome had got used to their premises in the barn and had almost forgotten how it used to be. Luckily Polly no longer talked about extending her livery yard to take over their barn, which had been her idea in the first place. She seemed content with the status quo and was still happy for Millie not to pay any rent in exchange for giving the horses their early feeds. Luckily the incompatible Amy rarely came to annoy them in their barn now she had Dragon to tame, although they suspected, by the rate at which the biscuits and chocolate bars disappeared from their jar, that she used it a fair bit when they were all at school. Her school lessons only took up two or three hours in the mornings and were often cancelled. What she was doing with Dragon no one quite knew but certainly she had been seen galloping over the top of the hill by Jake, once, and twice schooling rather wildly in the arena by Millie. Polly had washed her hands of her, considering Dragon a dangerous animal beyond redemption. If he killed her, she said, it would be at the door of the loopy psychiatrist who said a friend would be good for her.

But Millie couldn't help a sneaking sympathy for Amy. She knew herself how much pleasure she got from her darling Bluebell, ill-shaped and inadequate as he was, and she could see clearly how the gorgeous Dragon appealed to Amy. He was a challenge, and Amy rose to challenges. She challenged nearly everyone she met, as if wanting to be disliked, proud of it.

One afternoon Millie came home early from school and went down to the stable to take Bluebell out for a ride. Seeing Amy's bike in the yard, she went to Dragon's box to find her. It was an impulsive move, prompted by the feeling of guilt she harboured about the way the four of them had made no attempt lately to be friendly. She decided, nobly, to make the effort.

Amy was sitting in the straw in a corner of the box talking to Dragon, who stood with his nose amicably sniffing in her hair. When Millie looked over the door Dragon started back in surprise and Amy, looking up, said in her sour voice, 'What do *you* want?'

'I'm going for a ride. Do you want to come?'

Amy scowled, and grunted something undecipherable. Millie hadn't expected, that Amy's face would light up at the sight of her but the response was irritating.

'Suit yourself. I'm going to tack up.'

But when she came out on Bluebell she found Amy waiting for her on an impatient Dragon who was barging around in circles and scraping the new cobbles with an angry forefoot.

'Lead on,' she said, preferring to ride behind.

Amy went out and plunged Dragon straight into the river. He showed no hesitation although the water was high. Millie thought poor Bluebell might be swept away but, so eager was he to keep up with his new companion, he crashed after him, soaking Millie to the waist.

It was a raw winter day and Millie swore, cursing her stupid invitation, but her little pony seemed entranced by his new companion and belted after him. As Amy went straight into a gallop Millie had more to do than lament her discomfort, trying desperately to keep a safe path up the deep muddy ride, ducking the branches that threatened to decapitate her and skidding wildly round the twists and turns. Thinking of Polly, she started to laugh. How she would disapprove! Dragon was now out of sight with Bluebell even more frantic to keep up and Millie had no option but to sit it out. But she couldn't stop laughing.

Amy had kindly elected to wait for her at the top of the hill which was quite a surprise and Millie was able to pull up at last. Bluebell was really stirred up with the excitement and pranced about just like Dragon, wanting to gallop on.

'Do you always ride like that?'

'Yes. Mostly.' Amy cracked a smile. 'It's great on Dragon. Wild. He feels like – like that horse with wings – you know—'

'Pegasus.'

'Yes, like he could fly away.'

Millie thought of Polly, and dressage, and all she had been taught about riding safely in company — how aghast Polly would be if she knew! Crashing out of control across country was not on Polly's agenda, a different sort of riding altogether. It reminded Millie of those old prints you saw of hunting with horses upended in ditches and somersaulting over vast hedges: that was Amy's sort of riding. Somersaults were now called rotational falls in Polly's circle, she remembered, which rather made them sound like something you did on purpose. Amy was not of that mindset.

She asked her, as they walked (jiggled) towards the brow of the hill and the big house, 'Has Alex said any more about making a foursome with us for that dressage competition? You said you'd ask him.'

'Yes, I did. And he thinks it's great. He's working on it.'

'Really? The four of us, like you said?'

'Yeah. He's the hero and I'm the villain, and you and Imogen are the servants.'

That fitted.

'He didn't want you two in it at all. Just me and him, because of the horses. But I said you must be in it. So he said he'd create a part for lowly creatures, meaning Barney and Bluebell.'

Millie didn't know whether to be offended, or amazed that Amy had argued a place for them. She could see that it would be much easier to make a show with just the black horse and the white horse, both the same size and equally beautiful. Dragging in the two scruffs Barney and Bluebell would certainly down-grade any show.

'It's to music, he said. Sort of dressage and sort of pantomime.'

'I suppose Imogen and me are the pantomime?'

'Yes, I expect so.'

'But if you're the dressage, that'll be a laugh too.'

'Yes, it will. But he's going to train us, he said.'

Millie wished she hadn't asked. She had expected a surly answer in the negative but Amy, although not exactly tactful, had replied with goodwill and even a suspicion of hopeful anticipation. Had communing with her horse improved her outlook on life?

They skirted round the environs of the big house, looking over the gates into the stable yard. There was an elegant arch over the top with a clock tower set in it. The clock had stopped at five to three and its face was dappled with moss. It struck Millie that the yard was similar to their own in proportion and layout, but in much better condition. Theirs was probably by the same architect, working on a cheaper budget.

'It's an awful waste that it's not used any more,' Amy said. 'Why didn't Polly try to buy it instead of ours?'

'I think she tried, but it's not for sale.'

'It's tons nicer.'

Drier, Millie thought. Looking down on the river from the top of the hill she thought it was doubtful whether they would be able to cross it in a day or two. Thank goodness her own home stood proud on its little knoll. It was called Knoll Farm. It must have looked down on many floods in its lifetime.

Amy wanted to go on for miles but Millie had no wish to ride in the dark, especially as the weather was raw and the clouds were banking up ominously.

'You stay out if you like but I'm going home.'

They made a circle round the big house and through a few fields behind Emma's stables and headed back for the ford. Certainly the river was rising.

'I bet we won't be able to cross it by tomorrow.'

They crossed it and got soaked. They were lucky to get home. But Millie felt very contented with her ride.

Chapter 10

That night it started to rain heavily.

'Here we go,' grunted Mike Hodge, moving restlessly around in the front room from whose windows he could see his cattle sheds across the main road. They had flooded sometimes, although not very close to the river, and occasionally the road had been closed. But it was still open now, the headlights wavering in the rain, reflections doubling up the dancing patterns of light.

'Idiots,' he growled. 'The speed! — in this weather – they're all mad.'

They knew he would soon put on his heavy weather gear and go out to his sheds, and probably stay there all night.

Millie was worried about the horses. Jake was worried about his treasure, fidgeting with hope that Miss Brocklebank might drown. Susan Hodge was worried about Miss Brocklebank.

'I ought to go down.'

'Don't be so stupid,' said her husband. 'You know she won't budge. Save your breath. She's been offered help for years and won't take it.'

'All the same ...'

'You can come out to the sheds with me. We might have to move some of 'em and it needs two.'

'Very well, dear.'

Jake and Millie were given strict instructions to stay indoors.

'Don't you dare go down to the stables, whatever happens.

Ring that Polly Whatnot if you're worried about her horses. It's her problem.'

When they had gone Jake said, 'He wouldn't ask me to help. It makes me feel bad, that Mum has to go.'

'Oh, she knows it all backwards and you and I always make a hash of things. We just get his back up. Don't worry about it.'

'I couldn't be a farmer.'

'No, and he couldn't be anything else, so it doesn't matter.'

'I guess you're right.'

'I am.'

All the same, with nothing to do they couldn't settle. The rain fell more and more heavily and Millie couldn't help thinking of poor little Bluebell and Barney standing with their bedding squelching beneath them. She was sure the river must be in the stables by now and the big horses would be very nervous. The surface of Polly's arena would have floated away through the village. There was no way they could go to bed. Millie tried to ring Polly but there was no reply. Perhaps she was in the stables now? They tried to watch television, but after half an hour it went dead and all the lights went out. They looked out of the windows and there were no lights anywhere. Even the road had gone dead.

'The police must have closed it,' Jake said.

'It's weird.'

Millie went upstairs to look out of the top windows. There was a bit of a moon sometimes winking through the black cloud. On the road side there was no sign of life, but when she opened the window to look down on the river she was appalled to hear a thunderous roar of water. She had never heard the river before; the sound terrified her. She could glimpse that it was high, higher than she had ever seen it and its voice was evil. There was nothing sweet about the landscape below her. She screamed for Jake and he came blundering up the stairs, swearing in the dark.

'Look at the river!'

The curtains blew out horizontally from the open window, filling the room with the smell of the uncontainable water.

'Jake, the horses! And Miss Brocklebank! They'll all get swept away! It's never done this before.'

'Shut the window, idiot!'

She did so. It was better without the sound effects, but the capricious moon, showing for a second, showed a frightening scenario. Their house, on its knoll, was now surrounded by water. When they looked out at the front the road was now a river. The farm sheds on the other side stood proud, like their house, surrounded by water.

'It must be a flash flood. Crikey, I hope Mum and Dad are safe.'

'Jake, the horses! The ponies! We've got to let them out or they'll drown! And Miss Brocklebank—'

'We'll see if the phone's working.'

But it wasn't. Dead as a doornail.

'We can't leave it, Jake – we can't!'

'No. We'll try. But I'm not going to get drowned and nor are you. Maybe it's not so bad down there, where the water's got room to spread out. We'll go.'

They got their boots and anoraks and went out into the night. They stood at the garden gate, looking down but it was too hard to see just how much under water the stables were. They would find out by wading. It was true that the dreadful force of the rushing water that had echoed up into Millie's bedroom window was now somewhat alleviated as, once past the knoll, the river had room to spread across the water meadows. They came to the edge of the water halfway down the hill. It came lapping at their boots like the tide coming in, quite gently. They had to go in. They stood, hesitating a moment.

'If it's too high further down, Millie, we're not doing it,' Jake said.

Millie started to cry, thinking of dear little Bluebell and Barney unable to escape.

'We must, we must! And Miss Brocklebank.'

She started walking. The water soon flooded her boots, came up to her knees and then, freezingly, her bottom. She walked on. The ground levelled out slightly as they approached the garden, now a rippling lake. The cottage was in darkness, the water high up its walls. It was hard to make out, but it looked like the upstairs was still above the water-level. But for how long? Jake, in spite of wanting Miss Brocklebank to die, knew it was his responsibility to save her, dammit. Even if they got the horses out, they couldn't leave Miss Brocklebank.

By the time they got to the stable door the water was up to their waists. It was hard work wading against it, and harder work still to force the door open. The square yard had turned into a great lake.

'It's rising all the time,' Jake said. 'We've got to hurry.'

'What'll we do?'

Millie was feeling close to panic. Where to take the horses? There was nowhere.

'Just let them out,' Jake shouted. 'They'll go up the hill if they've any sense. Or drown.'

'Lead one perhaps and the others will follow.'

But what a hope! She could hear the kicking and whinnying going on in Polly's stable but she turned first to their own barn.

'I'll get Bluebell and Barney.'

She was gasping, half sobbing, with fright and rage at the difficulty before her, the freezing water tearing at her chest. It was definitely rising all the time. Luckily they always left the huge doors into their barn open and there were only the bars to take down to let the two ponies out. But all was silent in the stable part and although she couldn't see a thing she knew the ponies had gone. The bars that kept them in were broken. She felt for them. Yes, they were cracked across. Clever ponies, she thought, but where had they gone? The big gates into the driveway were always open so they could have gone anywhere. They must be barely on

90

their feet, the water so deep, but they hadn't met them as they came down the hill. Had the stupid things gone swimming?

'Oh Bluebell, Bluebell!' she sobbed.

But it was no good wasting time. Jake had already gone on to the other stable block where all the noise was coming from. Polly's newly built loose-boxes were strong and the doors were stoutly resisting the battering they were getting. Dragon's shrill whinny and crashing hooves were dominant; Red Sky was panicking but less noisily and Wake stood quiet. Sultan seemed terrified, cowering at the back of her box. The water was up to Millie's chest and she was beginning to panic herself, swimming not a strong suit.

'Just open the doors!' Jake shouted. 'They must fend for themselves'

They were almost swimming. She hauled on Dragon's door first and Jake came to help her: it was almost impossible against the weight of the water. But the two of them together heaved and when it was only a slit open the horse charged through, and went half galloping, half swimming, out of the main door, leaving Millie and Jake knocked off their feet and clinging desperately to the top-door grille. His departure started the other three horses neighing frantically, even the traumatised Sultan, and they set to, clinging together, to force the next door. This was Red Sky and she took a large bite out of Jake's shoulder as he strove to free her.

'Bitch! Bitch!' he shouted as she stormed out.

Millie knew she could never have done it alone. Jake was a rock and his strength equal to opening the doors, just. First Wake, who went with a snort, quite gently, not like the others and, luckily, was still in the main doorway when they managed to get Sultan's door open. At first Millie thought the mare wouldn't go, but she heard Wake give another snort and a whinny, as if he was calling her, and she went after him, a white ghost in the dark. And then together they disappeared.

'He waited for her!'

Millie was moved by Wake's behaviour, overwhelmed with relief now the job was done. Whatever happened to the horses next was beyond her and she thought they might well drown. Or would their animal sense steer them up to the high ground? They would not be able to see it in the dark. And where were the two ponies? They should have met them if they had turned that way. She was full of foreboding for them, perhaps, swept down the river. Her emotions were in turmoil. She felt Jake's arm grab her.

'You okay?'

'Yes.'

'We ought to get back, but—'

The water was up to their chests and not going away. Now the action was over Millie realised she was frozen to the bone, and could not stop shaking.

'Miss Brocklebank?'

'Yeah, the old fool.'

'Oh, Jake, what can we do?'

'That cottage will fall apart with the force of the water. Even if she is upstairs she's in danger. I wanted her to die, but now it comes to the point – it's all different.'

They were standing in the open yard, the water lapping all round them.

Jake said, 'Our car – our boat. It might be the answer.'

'You're crazy! It doesn't work.'

'Who said? We've never had it in the water yet. I bet you anything it's afloat now. We could use it ourselves, at least. We'll be swimming here in five minutes at the rate the water's rising.'

It was true. Millie was fighting down panic. The water was holding her off her feet, right up to her armpit, and only by Jake taking her arm and pulling her was she able to cross the yard, half swimming, trying desperately to be brave. What had their parents said about not leaving the house? Of the horses there was no sign.

Her brother was right. Their car-boat was in the doorway.

trying to get out but unable to, because it was diagonally across. It hit Millie in the chest and she laid her arms over it and her spirits soared as she felt it lift her off her feet, strong and sound.

'It works!'

'We want some light! I'll try and find the torch– I know it's on the shelf, high up. It should still be there. Here, I'll bunk you on. Give me a leg.'

The next minute she was dragging herself out of the water on to the deck of the weird machine she and Imogen had so derided. How wrong they had been! It felt to her like an ocean liner, stout and safe beneath her.

'Don't stand up, lie still.'

Millie lay panting, shaking across the rough boards, while Jake went swearing into the darkness. There were some crashes and splashes and vile curses and then Millie saw a light glimmer above the water, revealing the extraordinary scene.

A flash flood, surely, as seen on television? Certainly no ordinary flood. The water was right up the walls now and Jake got back swimming, holding the torch high. It was a wind-up, made for uncivilised situations. Jake climbed aboard to join Millie and wound it up until it gave out a strong, violet light. The scene was so weird they just sat there taking stock.

'It depends if there's much current outside, whether we can reach the cottage,' Jake said. 'It's okay in here, but it's quite likely when we're out of the yard we'll just get swept down to the village. In which case we can tell someone else to go and save the old girl.'

'Won't it sink?'

'No. Feel it – it's quite steady. But sit still, and keep down. I've got the pitchfork to try and punt it. And with luck the outboard might go, once we're out of the yard. Although I know there's hardly any petrol in it. But let's hand it out of the doorway. It'll go, once it's square on. We measured it, to make sure we could get it out.'

They used their hands to push themselves out of the doorway and tried to make for the big open gateway that gave on to the drive. The current was pushing them that way and with the pitchfork Jake managed to guide it to the opening. Millie half lay, winding the torch to keep the light going.

'Hold on here and I'll see if the outboard'll start. It'll be against the current to get back to the cottage. It's our only chance.'

'What if it won't?'

'We'll just have to go with it down to the bridge and stop it there. If we can.'

Millie clung desperately to the gatepost while beneath her the ramshackle vehicle was pulled strongly by the current. Jake kept pulling the outboard string, causing the engine to cough and whirr. He was swearing terribly.

'It does go. We've had it going. Harry can always work it.'

Millie lay there, her hands getting torn by the rough timber she clutched on to for her life. Her whole body was shaking with cold and fright; at least Jake was getting warm by his efforts with the outboard. The torch faded, losing the bizarre landscape of grim water which was once their pretty water meadows. The sky was as black as the water and large raindrops were throwing themselves down, almost bouncing on the newly formed lake. The car-boat at least felt firm and strong beneath them, although it was trying its hardest to get free from its constraints, and its deck was not completely above water. It lay about three inches under and little wavelets broke around Millie's prone body. She wondered if Miss Brocklebank would be waiting for them on the roof of her cottage, sitting beside the chimney. She doubted very much if this rescue was going to happen, but thought they would have no trouble in whizzing down into the village.

To her amazement the engine suddenly burst into life.

'Blimey!'

Jake was as surprised as she was.

'Let go! Let go!'

Jake fell back as the car-boat seemed to leap through the gateway. It didn't go straight but turned in circles as if in some strange dance. They could make out the bulk of the stable yard, which they needed to go round to get to the cottage. Jake fiddled with the engine controls and got it into gear, which stopped it turning and gave it the merest forward movement against the current. It took them down the side of the stable yard to the edge of Polly's arena, where it got hung up on the fence that surrounded it. The engine caught and was nearly wrenched off.

'Hang on to the fence, Millie! Hold it against the current.'

Hanging on seemed to be her role in life. Her hands were numb and scored with splinters, but she managed to stop the car-boat's eagerness to go downstream. The fence trembled beneath them.

'Push it off! Push it off!'

She hardly had any strength left. Jake pushed with his feet and the car-boat came free. The little engine just held it against the current, moving upstream inch by inch. The cottage loomed before them, still in one piece, with the water up to the bedroom windowledge.

'She can just step out. Thank goodness. It should be quite easy.'

There was a lee beside the cottage against the full force of the current and they managed to hold on to a drainpipe. Millie couldn't believe they had managed to come this far, but the thought of Miss Brocklebank sitting on their car-boat hurtling down towards the village started to give her the giggles.

'Miss Brocklebank!' Jake roared.

'Miss Brocklebank!' squeaked Millie.

'Perhaps she's died of fright,' Jake said. 'I hope so.'

'Jake!'

They roared together, hanging on to the drainpipe. No answer.

'She's died,' Jake said hopefully.

But then a voice came from the window, 'What do you want, dears?'

'We've come to rescue you!'

'I don't want rescuing, thank you. I'm quite all right. The bed is still above water.'

The disembodied voice floated out of the window. They pictured the old girl sitting up in her flannel pyjamas, cool as a cucumber.

'The cottage might collapse, Miss Brocklebank.'

'Oh rubbish, dear. Why should it?'

Jake said softly, 'Because it's as old and rickety as you are, you old hen.'

Millie started to laugh, mainly with relief at the prospect of not having to have Miss Brocklebank join them aboard.

'Leave her! We've tried.'

'We'll try to get help to you, Miss Brocklebank, if you won't come.'

'That's very kind, but I'm quite all right.'

'Are you sure?'

It wasn't as if Jake didn't try. Millie realised he wanted her out of the place badly, so he could dig up her garden as soon as the water receded, but it was not to be.

'You're very kind, dear, but I'm quite all right.'

'She's a lunatic.'

'If we don't have to rescue her, we could go home, not have to whizz down to the village.'

'Yeah.'

The thought of home, proudly snug and dry above the waters, was suddenly overpoweringly inviting. They were both cold to the bone and exhausted. They had done their best and had only themselves to bother about now. If Miss Brocklebank was choosing to die, so be it.

'We can aim for the knoll, but it will be against the current – we might not make it.'

'We can jump off and wade.'

'It's too deep here. Start praying, Millie.'

Perhaps they would end up whizzing down to the village after all. The little engine spluttered manfully and Jake shoved off from the cottage and headed for home. Millie tried to punt with the pitchfork but couldn't touch bottom. Anxiety flooded back: they had achieved so much, not to make the final landing would be heart-breaking. Besides, Millie thought the horses would be up there, waiting for her. They had more sense than to drown themselves, surely?

'Oh Jake – it must—!'

'She's making it, just.' She could hear the note of pride in his voice. 'Wish Harry could see it.'

He had forgotten about the petrol. Millie had just found she could touch bottom with the pitchfork when the engine stopped.

'Crikey Millie, jump for it! Jump!'

Jake snatched the pitchfork from her hands and stuck it hard into the water and pushed Millie off the uphill side. The shock made her scream. She went under but immediately found her feet were touching bottom. She struggled wildly, half wading, half swimming, until she found herself more and more out of the water, until it was only up to her waist. She turned round and found Jake behind her, pushing the car-boat in front of him.

'Help me – pull it up. I don't want – want to lose it.'

She turned and pulled. Together they managed to beach it some fifty metres from their garden gate. As they dragged it out of the water they became aware of large black shapes snorting and snuffling around them.

Millie was suddenly ecstatic.

'The horses! Jake, the horses! They're here!'

'Bloody things!'

Red Sky had bitten him again. Millie started to laugh, a touch hysterically.

'It's fantastic! We've done it, Jake. They're safe.'

Eyes now well accustomed to the dark, or perhaps a glimmer of moonlight, showed her the familiar shapes, the four horses in their smart, sodden winter rugs standing on the edge of the great

lake that stretched right down to the village. Lights were shining by the bridge, no doubt emergency lights, car headlight perhaps, but otherwise there was no other light anywhere. Their own house stood proud on its own hill, well-named Knoll Farm. They stood, exhausted, taking it all in. The cattle sheds across the road were still above water too, so they knew their parents were safe. But of the two ponies there was no sign.

'Oh, poor Bluebell – Barney—?'

'They'll be okay. Ponies like that – they know how to look after themselves.'

'Why didn't they come this way?'

'They're only small. I expect they were swept off their feet. But they can swim. Ponies can swim. They're probably safe in the village.'

'Oh, they must be! They must be!'

But there was nothing they could do about it now. Millie was so exhausted that she lay for a moment against Wake's neck, her arms round him, trying to regain her strength. At least these four were safe from the water and Dragon and Red Sky were already grazing as if nothing was amiss. Wake walked up the hill to the farm's gate, Millie holding on to his mane, Sultan coming close behind, and Jake opened it to let Millie through.

'What a sweetie,' Millie said. 'He's looking after me.'

'He wants to come in the kitchen,' Jake said sourly. 'Watch it!'

He slammed the gate shut. Wake stood with his head over snatching at the blackberry bushes, apparently not the least perturbed by his night's adventure, and Millie and Jake scurried up to the house. Pushing open the kitchen door they felt lovely warmth wafting out to embrace them.

'Oh, what bliss!'

The house, apart from there being no electricity, was gorgeously apart from all the mayhem surrounding it. They could even run hot baths, and boil the kettle on the Aga.

'If only Mum and Dad could get back! When it gets light

perhaps I could get across to them in our boat. Dad's got a can of petrol in the garage.'

'The water might go down as quickly as it came up. Perhaps we could put a light in the front window to show them we're okay. The storm lantern's in the cupboard under the stairs.'

'Yeah, good idea. And when Miss Brocklebank gets taken away I'm going to dig up the leek bed. It's the chance of a lifetime.'

'But what if she won't go?'

'She'll have to, kicking and screaming. They'll never let her stay. It's much too dangerous.'

'The cottage could well collapse. But we did our best, after all. Thank goodness she refused to come. We might never have made it with three of us.'

'We tried, at least.'

They had hot baths, made cocoa, and, eventually, went to bed. But it was impossible to sleep, thinking of their parents marooned with the cattle and old Miss Brocklebank in her bedroom. Millie got up once or twice and looked out but the water seemed to be no lower. She thought she could make out the shapes of the four horses in the darkness grazing, quite happily it seemed, just outside the farm's gate, but there was no other sign of life, not on the road nor in the village. She slept fitfully, and then heavily towards dawn when a shaft of sunlight came creeping over her pillow.

Dazed, she remembered slowly all that had happened. That Bluebell was missing was the worst of her memories ... Miss Brocklebank refusing help ... She slid out of bed, stiff and sore, to see what daylight was revealing.

The water had gone down quite considerably although it still covered the meadows below and lapped through the stable yard. But where Miss Brocklebank's cottage had been there was nothing but a heap of rubble sticking up out of the current and the tops of her runner beans sticks waving in the breeze as if to summon help.

Chapter 11

'Jake! Jake!' Millie screamed.

She raced out of her bedroom and flung open Jake's door. He wasn't there, his bed rumpled, the duvet flung back. She ran to the top of the stairs and then realised that there were voices coming up from below, the familiar sound of her father shouting, the smell of bacon cooking … just like a normal day. She couldn't believe it. How long had she slept? What was happening?

She went to the top of the stairs and her mother stood below, staring anxiously up.

'It's all right, Millie. Come down. We're all safe. Everything is all right.'

'Miss Brocklebank! Her house has gone!'

'She was rescued, pet. They came for her.'

Jake yelled up at her: 'In a helicopter, Millie! Just think – the old girl got winched up, kicking and screaming! I saw it. It was terrific.'

'When it got light they sent a helicopter, just in time,' her mother said. 'Jake's told me all about your effort to help her and the silly old biddy wouldn't come. All for the best, as it turned out. But you did well – thank goodness you didn't get swept away. I was so worried – I guessed you would go for the horses …' Her voice faded and Millie realised she looked as haggard as she herself felt: wiped out, exhausted. The night had been horrific. Only Jake seemed to be thriving on the excitement. Millie knew he was triumphant at seeing Miss Brocklebank removed. He could start digging as soon as the water receded. No wonder he was laughing.

And it seemed that her father had something to laugh about too.

'The bridge into the village has collapsed into the river. No traffic! And I doubt if it'll be rebuilt in a hurry. What bliss!'

'We waded home as soon as the water started to go down,' Susan Hodge told Millie. 'I was so worried about you.'

In the midst of all the excitement Millie's mind went back to the little ponies, Bluebell and Barney, swooshed away into the darkness, and she tried to stop the tears coming. Of course they would be safe somewhere … why think otherwise? She could call Amy to look for them in the village. Call her on her mobile.

But Jake was ahead of her. 'Your friend Polly called to see what's happened to her horses. She was demented. I told her they were grazing outside our front door. I told her to look for Barney and Bluebell and she said she would. She can't get up here as the police have sealed the road off. I told her to get a wet-suit and swim up but her reply was rather rude.'

Millie knew Jake was euphoric with the knowledge that his way was clear to dig up his treasure, but now all the excitement was over all she could think about was what might have happened to Bluebell and Barney. The glow of pride that she had experienced by saving Polly's four horses was now totally obliterated by worry over the ponies. Her mother tried to cheer her up as they all sat round the table drinking tea and making toast and watching their father tuck into his home-made beef burgers, three in six slices of toast. Why didn't he get fat? 'Because my life is one long worry, that's why,' he always said, but for once he was laughing.

'The road is out! Peace at last. I can buzz backwards and forwards all day long. Long may it remain so.'

They had never seen him so happy. Jake was the same. Millie realised it was only herself who had not profited from the flood. She tried to tell herself the ponies were bound to be safe somewhere round the village; ponies could swim, after all. She tried to ring Amy but Amy's phone was silent. She must be worried about Dragon, surely? But no one could reach Knoll Farm without a boat. They could hardly expect a visit.

Jake was watching what was going on through a pair of binoculars. He reported a mass of police by the bridge, mostly just standing around, and a couple of JCBs starting to clear the rubble. The ruins of the bridge were impeding the flow and the build-up of water was still flooding the houses nearest to the bridge. Most of the village had turned out to stare at the disaster.

'They're not going to clear that up in a hurry,' said Mike Hodge, taking a look.

'Great.'

'We can't get to school,' Jake said. Yet Millie knew he couldn't wait for the water to recede from Miss Brocklebank's garden.

'They'll make a temporary bridge, surely?' Susan Hodge asked. 'We can't be cut off for long – what about shopping, let alone school?'

'Someone's coming,' Jake said.

'What do you mean?'

'In a kayak, paddling like fury. It's your friend Amy. The police are shouting at her but she's taking no notice.'

'Show me.'

Millie snatched the binoculars from Jake and focused them on what looked like a water-beetle creeping along the edge of the flood. Yes, she could see it was Amy and no doubt Amy could see her dear Dragon grazing safely on the hill. Where on earth had she got the kayak from? Someone's back garden, no doubt.

'Does no one care for that child?' Susan Hodge asked in despair. 'She's putting her life at risk in that little boat.'

Millie thought she put her life at risk every time she mounted her horse, but she put on her coat and went out to meet her. Her mother shouted after her to bring her in but Millie pretended not to hear. At least Amy could go back and look for Bluebell and Barney. Perhaps she could go back with her? But the kayak was a single-seater. Amy ran it on to the grass and sat panting.

l'I – I – was so worried —'

'Who lent you the boat?'

'Oh, nobody, really. I just borrowed it. Was it you who got the horses out?'

'Me and Jake. But Bluebell and Barney got swept away. Can you look for them? They must be round the village somewhere, the way the current took them.'

Amy slithered out of the kayak and pulled it up on to the grass. She was soaked through.

'I just wanted to see Dragon. He's all right here for a bit, isn't he? Your father won't mind? There's plenty of grass for them.'

'Yes. But you will go and look for the ponies? I'll look after Dragon if you go and look for Bluebell and Barney.'

'Yes, okay. It's deal.'

All four horses had come over to see what was going on and Amy fussed Dragon for a few minutes. Millie dutifully asked her to come in the house but luckily she refused and soon set off the way she had come, the kayak speeding away on the current. Millie hoped she would be able to stop before arriving in the arms of the police, and prayed that she would remember the deal. If only she could get down to the village herself …

She watched for a few minutes and saw Amy beach herself well clear of the police, on the opposite side to where they were all working. She then just left the kayak stuck in the reeds, not bothered about returning it to the back garden from where she had no doubt discovered it, and disappeared into the village. Millie feared she had already forgotten about her part of the bargain. It occurred to her to ring the police to enquire about the ponies when she got back into the house, but they seemed to be continually engaged so there was no luck there. Her mother was cross she hadn't brought Amy back with her.

The next visit was, not unexpectedly, from Polly. Instead of a kayak Polly had appropriated an extremely smart motor-boat which was driving to Knoll Farm from the opposite direction. The boat circled the knoll with much panache, sliding sideways on the current and then bucking into it with a powerful roar of two huge outboard motors. It appeared to be Alex at the wheel, kitted out in white oilskins with FASTNET in large letters across the back, and Polly sitting shouting directions, dressed in equally smart crossing-the-Atlantic gear. The horses of course took great exception to this intrusion upon their peace and started bucking and kicking round the edge of their domain, churning up great clods of wet earth. Alex had the sense to slow down but then the boat started slipping away downstream so he had to charge it up again. He gingerly circled the farm and came to rest on the front drive, as near as he could get to the house. He gallantly jumped out, crotch deep, and held the boat while Polly dismounted, then tied it with a long rope to the plum tree outside the front door. By this time Mike Hodge was at the threshold ready to give them a broadside about causing the horses to mash up his fields, but Polly was ahead of him with a display of overwhelming charm, fluttering eyelashes and copious thanks for rescuing her horses. Susan Hodge invited them in and sat them, steaming, beside the Aga and Millie told them how she and Jake had rescued their animals. Her father stood listening, obviously thrown by Alex's glamour (for a man!!!) and stunned by the thick layer of Polly's charm. If only he knew, Millie thought, how bitchy she could be! How she could turn it on!

'It's impossible to move them until the water goes down but I will reimburse you for the damage they are doing to your grass, and of course we've brought a supply of feed to see them through. If dear Millie could feed them for us …' – a simpering smile in Millie's direction – 'And then when it's possible we'll take them away. I'm afraid there's no way of getting a horsebox here because both the bridges are down and you are totally cut off.'

'What do you mean, both the bridges?'

'The bridge into the village, and the bridge upstream of it where your road leaves the motorway. There'll be no traffic past you for some time, I imagine.'

'God in Heaven! Peace at last! What brilliant news! Get the sloe gin out, Susan, we must drink to this!'

Never had Millie seen her father so happy. She couldn't imagine exactly what it meant for them: peace, certainly, but how did they get to school, go shopping, live? Isolated on their island … how strange. Her mother, rummaging for the sloe gin, looked worried, but her father was euphoric. He poured large glasses of sloe gin all round, in spite of knowing that only a small glass made them all drunk. They used it only at Christmas and it was powerful stuff, made by Susan herself.   After a few sips Millie forgot all about Bluebell and Barney, her mother started making another breakfast, plying Polly and Alex with bacon sarnies and her father got out his photo album and started showing the visitors the portraits of his prize-winning bulls which all looked exactly the same (except to him) and prompted Polly to summon from her inside pocket a wallet of photos of herself doing intricate dressage on Red Sky. Heads together, they talked over each other, laughing and exclaiming, while Alex charmed Susan with a long tale about his career in modelling – the Fastnet gear was a relic from a modelling stint at the Boat Show. Susan thought a catwalk was something to do with showing cats, which misinterpretation caused much hilarity.

'Have another glass!'

'Drunk in charge of a motor-boat – we must be careful!'

But they weren't. Eventually, when Mike Hodge fell asleep over his photo album and his wife dropped the hot grill pan in the dog's basket , Alex and Polly pulled themselves together to take their leave. Jake and Millie helped them unload the horse feed out of the boat. Polly then thought to ask where Barney and Bluebell were, at which Millie burst into tears and said 'Drowned!'

and Polly hugged her in a uncharacteristically maternal fashion and assured her, as had everyone else, that they would turn up. And then, fast sobering up in the cold morning air, she had to examine her own horses to see that they were all unharmed. Red Sky bit her and Sultan wouldn't come near. Kindly Wake stayed by Sultan and Dragon wandered away as far as he could and started pawing at the water.

'Their rugs are all soaking, but what can I do? I don't know when we'll be able to fetch them.'

Millie reassured her. 'They're quite all right here for the time being. I'll feed them, don't worry.'

And with this sudden display of mutual affection Polly and Alex sailed away. After they had gone Jake said, 'Well, they could have fed the horses before they went. Leaving it all to you!' and Millie said, 'I'll feed them later.'

Polly had made no mention of helping look for the ponies and all Millie could do was pray that Amy and Imogen would be searching round the village for some sign of them.

As it was, feeling very peculiar, she went inside and joined her slumbering parents in the kitchen.

Chapter 12

By the time Millie went tearfully to bed she had received reports back from both Imogen and Amy (separately) that in spite of extensive searching they had found no trace of the ponies. No one had seen them. The police had not heard of them. In her imagination Millie kept seeing their poor little bodies stretched out lifeless on the riverbank somewhere and nothing would console her. She went out and fed the beastly horses that had survived with Polly's copious supplies, and then went to bed.

The water was rapidly receding. In the morning the horses had quite a lot more grazing and it was clear that by evening the river would be back in its proper place.

Jake was fizzing with excitement.

'I can start digging tonight. I'll go out when Mum and Dad have gone to bed. I'll ring Harry to come.'

Their parents went out in the tractor in the afternoon to see to the cattle and Jake and Millie decided to go down to the stable yard. The horses would have to go back. Millie only hoped their owners would come and see to them, for there was all the wet bedding to be removed which would take ages. They put their gumboots on and went down the hill. The horses followed them and stopped to eat Miss Brocklebank's vegetables while Millie and Jake went into the stable yard. Millie went to fetch the horses' headcollars and Jake went into the barn.

The stables looked terrible with a layer of mud and river-scum lying over everything. Millie took it in with a sinking heart.

Surely the others would be coming to help? The horses would have to go in as, with the water fast disappearing, there was nothing to stop them taking off into the far countryside. Luckily Miss Brocklebank's vegetables were keeping them occupied for the time being. The poor garden looked terrible and the cottage was just a heap of junk, Miss Brocklebank's bed with its pink candlewick counterpane sat proudly on top of a heap of bricks that had once been the chimney. The strong earthy smell of provoked nature drifted across the pastures, and an evening mist was spreading over the water. It was eerily quiet, the road silent, no wind to stir the sodden trees which hung in defeated swags along the bank. Totally depressing in the fading light: Millie shivered, depression swamping her.

Suddenly there was a shout from the barn. 'Millie! Millie ! Come and look!'

Something to do with his stupid treasure, no doubt ... what a maniac he was! She turned towards the barn and saw him standing there, grinning and laughing.

'You'll never guess! Come and look!'

She hurried across, infected by the tenor of his voice, and stepped into the barn. A familiar whicker came to her ears and there were Bluebell and Barney standing in their quarters just as if they had never been away, eating the wet straw but pausing momentarily to give her a welcome.

'Jake!' Her voice choked in amazement. She thought she must be dreaming. Of all the places she had never thought to look ... the most obvious, when one gave it a thought. They had come home, as any sensible animal would. She rushed across the barn and flung her arms round dear Bluebell, burying her face in his stinky wet mane, half laughing, half crying. Barney came pushing in, wanting a welcome too.

'I bet they've been here for ages,' Jake said. 'I don't suppose they floated very far.'

'I'll clean out their stable first.'

'Can't you get the other horses in first? Then I can start digging.'

'We can't put them in their boxes the way they are—'

And then, suddenly, there were voices outside in the yard ... thank the stars! The others had arrived, help was at hand – she wouldn't have to clean all the stables out herself.

Jake groaned 'They'll be here all night ...'

It was Polly, Joe and Alex, having walked round the back way on the other side of the river and crossed by the footbridge. Polly was the only dry one, having been given a piggyback by the noble Joe, the footbridge still being half a metre under water. While they were still groaning at the sight of their once pristine loose-boxes, Imogen and Amy arrived, having been given a lift across the river by the police, and then Harry turned up, having spotted Amy's kayak in the rushes and making use of it. Everyone was talking and laughing and crashing about looking for pitchforks and wheelbarrows. The horses were brought in from outside and tied up to await the cleaning of their quarters.

Jake and Harry watched crossly as their spades were appropriated.

'They'll be here all night!'

'We've got all night,' said Harry equably. 'My mum thinks I'm sleeping over with you.'

'Good. Millie can tell Mum when she goes home that I've gone back with you.'

The clean-up process became rather like a party, everyone exchanging tales of their experiences, and buoyed up with the relief of finding all the horses unharmed.

It was hard work cleaning out the floors, the pile of wet straw growing ever higher, but even Amy did some work and Jake and Harry eventually joined in, trundling barrows, seeing that the quicker the job got done the sooner they could get to work outside. There was dry hay on the top of the stacked bales – the bottom ones ruined of course (lucky Polly was so rich!) – so haynets were filled, dry rugs produced and soon the horses were back eating as if nothing had happened, possibly quite pleased with their unusual outing. Millie had no way of knowing what had happened to the two ponies: perhaps they had been at home all the while Amy and Imogen had been searching round the village.

Millie and Jake were dying to say 'I told you so' when Polly moaned about her arena floating away, instead Jake said rather sharply, 'What about your poor old auntie floating away as well?' which shut her up, and then she had to hear of their dramatic attempt at rescue. It didn't appear as if she had made anything but a cursory enquiry about where her old aunt had been taken but she did say she would have to see about finding her somewhere else to live. More pressing to her mind was finding a better situation for her horses.

'This could happen again!'

'It's never been as bad as this before,' Millie pointed out. 'Only a few inches over the floor in the stables and Miss Brocklebank's cottage, never in the barns.'

'I was wondering about that stable yard up the hill, behind Standing Hall. It's doing nothing, after all. That's a very nice yard. Of course I did ask Emma if we could come back, temporarily, but she was downright unpleasant. Made me absolutely determined to beat her in the festival in the summer. In the dressage event.'

'Oh, we're going in for that, aren't we, girls?'

Alex was sitting on one of the feed-bins still dressed in his Fastnet gear with a pair of shining waders hitched up over his bottom. He grinned at Millie and Imogen and appealed to Amy, 'That right, Amy? You and me starring and the ponies for back-up.'

'Yes,' said Amy. 'It's a bullfight. Dragon and me's the fighting bull and Alex's the matador. We dance – that's the dressage bit – and then he kills me.'

'Blimey!' Jake exclaimed. Then, seeing that Millie and Imogen were struck dumb by this news, he asked, 'Where do the ponies come in?'

'They are spectators. They prance around while we're fighting.'

'Prance around?' snorted Imogen. 'What's that supposed to mean?'

'In the background, quietly. Everyone will be watching Alex and me.'

Millie exchanged goggle-eyes with Imogen at this news – when had they been consulted? – while Polly's hackles rose instantly at the idea of this taking place in direct competition to her planned duo with Joe.

'When did you plan all this? No thought to liaise with anyone else?'

'Just an idea,' Alex said airily. 'Anyone can enter. The winner is the best entertainment for the crowd, I thought. Just because it's turned into a dressage competition between Emma and her pals doesn't mean to say anyone else can't have a go.'

'If Amy thinks she's going to get that horse doing anything as advanced as some sort of a dressage spectacular between now and the summer she's even crazier than I thought.'

'I've got all day,' Amy said smugly. 'Dragon is my therapy.'

'Bully for you. Just don't make out, the two of you, that you are pupils of mine.'

'We're not,' Alex pointed out, 'Only liveries. Don't get miffed. Our show will be totally different from yours.'

'I bet it will, if you think Dragon and Sultan can approach anything Joe and I can do.'

Deciding to join in the row Imogen said frostily, 'And this prancing about Millie and I have got to do, who's choreographing that?'

'I am,' said Alex. 'You will love it, dears. I thought the ponies could wear beautiful caparison thingies, all embroidered like knights, down to their heels, so whatever they do underneath won't show.'

'And Millie and I can wear burkas so no one can see how ugly we are?'

'No, dear, I thought Spanish dress to go with the theme. Those wonderful frilly dresses and mantillas on your heads.'

'I'm going to wear bull's horns,' said Amy.

'I thought Dragon was the bull.'

'Me and Dragon, as one—'

'This is completely downgrading dressage into a circus routine,' Polly said.

'But circus routine is all pirouettes and dancing – flying changes to you – and Spanish trot … what's the difference?'

Jake and Harry could see that this argument was going to go on all night. Imogen and Millie were obviously furious at being downgraded to 'jiggling about', Polly was in one of her strops, poor Joe was trying to look as if he had nothing to do with her and Amy was in her usual 'I'm right, don't argue with me' mood. Enough to make anyone want to crash her on the head with a spade. Harry cleverly went to the fuse box and pulled the trip so all the lights went out, which broke up the conversation and everyone started blundering about trying to get themselves together to leave. Millie got the torch and went out to the main stable to show everyone their horses were settled. Polly and Alex were still arguing outside and Amy had slipped away on her own as usual. Joe was just standing saying goodnight to Wake. Millie told him how good Wake was when they let them out in the flood, how he waited for Sultan.

'He's much the nicest horse of these four.'

'Yes, too good for me. I'd rather just mess about with him – you know, enjoy it like you all do – but Polly, she's such a nagger.'

'Well, at least she showed you how nice it is to have a horse. After she's got this competition out of the way you can say you want to do something different. Go hunting, that would be great. Stand up to her.'

'Yeah, perhaps.' He didn't sound too confident. He really was a nerd. A nice one, but … what a load of weirdos Polly's liveries were … when they had all gone it was quite a relief to be left with the two boys and Imogen. Thank goodness everything was back to normal.

One adventure over and the next one about to start. The boys had their spades back and took the wind-up lantern off Millie. Millie wanted to stay but Jake said she had to go home else their parents would get suspicious. Imogen too.

The two girls went to say goodnight to their ponies. No one would know anything untoward had happened now.

But Imogen said, 'Blooming cheek, telling us we've got to jiggle about while they do all the grandstanding. We'll think of something, Millie. Surprise 'em all. Barney and Bluebell. Manky and Wonky.'

They both started to laugh.

'We'll beat the lot.'

Millie started for home up the hill. It seemed life was going to get harder than ever. Once Imogen had set her mind on something, she could outdo the lot of them.

Chapter 13

In spite of being so tired, Millie found it hard to sleep. She wished she could have stayed with Jake and Harry to see if their hopes might be rewarded; it would have kept her mind off the worrying prospect of being forced into a gruesome competition in the summer, which sounded as if it could only result in a terrible public humiliation. Why ever had Imogen risen to the bait, instead of just saying no thank you? Now that they had got the ponies back Millie just wanted to lie there happily thinking how lucky she was but, as usual, there was now something else to worry about.

She had no idea what time Jake would come home. Digging in the dark would be difficult, although the ground would be soft enough. Poor old Miss Brocklebank! It didn't seem as if she would get much joy from her niece: probably be dumped in the cheapest old people's home. She would die without her garden. Something else to take on board, not to let her be manoeuvred by Polly. Millie guessed her mother would take a hand. She then wondered how on earth Jake would get home unnoticed in the middle of the night, no doubt covered in mud. Perhaps tomorrow they would be millionaires!

At last she slept.

Jake couldn't believe his luck in having Miss Brocklebank's garden at his mercy. No traffic on the road, no one to see their lantern, just good old Harry as keen as himself. It was a still night with a half moon giving quite a fair light when it appeared at intervals out of the clouds. The eyes quickly became accustomed, and it was good to get to work and warm up. The garden hard against the stable wall where they wanted to dig was planted with a forest of leeks and waist-high Brussels sprouts but with the ground so soft they came out easily. Jake could not help feeling bad as he heaved at their roots – the poor old girl ... but if it all came out right she would be lovely and rich. What if it didn't? – not to be considered. The dank sour smell of Brussels sprouts rose into the night air.

'Wish I had gloves,' Harry complained. 'Hope you're going to give me a cut if this works out. You get half and the old girl gets half, is that the rule?'

'Yes, as far as I know.'

'Get the machine out again and see if it's still interested. We might have got all there was, just a few little bits. We don't want to work for nothing.'

Jake had so convinced himself that he had found treasure that he hadn't thought to use the machine again. Realising how stupid he was, he went and fetched it from the barn. Luckily it had been on the top of the old cupboard where the girls stored their horsey things and had survived the flood and, amazingly, still worked. Sick with trepidation, Jake switched it on over the cleared patch of earth. After all his dreams, surely it was going to give him some joy? Or was the treasure now firmly embedded under Polly's concrete?

But no. It was beeping faintly. He circled cautiously, following where the noise grew stronger.

'Here, by the leeks,' Harry said. 'Come down a bit.'

He wasn't mistaken. The noise was quite certain, stronger than it had been in the stable.

'Fantastic!'

The further he went into the leeks the louder it got.

'Oh, come on, let's get digging!'

They dug the leeks out as carefully as they could and made a tidy pile and then attacked the wet soil.

'Not too hard – it might be quite fragile, whatever's under there.'

Their feet slithered in the mud as they carried spadefuls of earth out of the area, trying, in spite of their eagerness, to be methodical and tidy. They were soon sweating, swearing, laughing. Miss Brocklebank's good husbandry meant that the soil was easy to work, few stones to stop the spades, no old bricks. If they hit something it would surely be treasure? Digging out large spadefuls, they stopped to examine each one by the inadequate light of the lantern to see if anything was embedded there; their hands and fingers froze with the crumbling and breaking up.

'Here.' Harry felt something hard. 'No. A stone.'

He thrust the spade in again.

'Steady on,' Jake said. 'Listen, something hard. Be careful.'

Harry withdrew the spade and Jake put his hand down the split it had made. Waggling his fingers round he came against something metallic. Not a stone. Another wretched horseshoe? Ancient bottle opener? This is where the metal detector had been at its loudest. He got his fingers round the object and pulled it out. While he stood squidging the wet earth off it Harry knelt down and fished about for more.

'There's lots,' he said. 'Bits.'

The two of them knelt down and scrabbled with their hands. It was true: there was a cache of objects, some quite large curved bits and button-shaped pieces, and pins and unidentifiable lumps of what felt like bronze or iron. Or gold? Jake was breathless with excitement.

'I'll fetch a bucket to put them in and we can go and look in the light.'

He fetched a bucket from the stable and they dropped the pieces in. Harry fixed the spade in the earth to mark the spot and they retired back to the stable and put the light on. Harry put the bucket under the tap and covered the stuff with water to clean it and they took brushes from the grooming kits and sat on the floor to brush the objects clean. The horses watched them benignly over their doors, chewing hay, snuffling softly and blinking in the unaccustomed light.

'This piece is like the first bit I found,' Jake said. 'It had a sort of serpent engraved down it and so has this.'

'This bit is a sort of hinge or something. It opens and shuts.'

'And there's a bracelet, look – something like a bracelet ..'

'And this is only one handful --- there must be lots more …'

They laid the bits out as they cleaned them on the floor and sat gazing in admiration, trying to surmise what this find might mean for them.

'I'm sure it's the real thing,' Jake said. 'We must do the rest in daylight so we can see what we're doing. It's hopeless in the dark. I'll take this home with me and I suppose I shall have to tell my parents about it. I wasn't sure until tonight but I'm sure now. I knew! I knew it was for real.'

'It's great.'

Harry yawned, remembered he was supposed to staying over at Jake's.

'I've got to come with you. I can't go home.'

It was long past midnight. They tidied up and put out the light and set off up to the knoll with the bucket of findings. They were wet and cold and covered in mud but gripped with excitement, laughing and chattering, and when they went indoors, although they tried to keep quiet, it was impossible. The dogs barked, sensing the unusual tension. Jake fell over the log basket and spilled their bucket of treasure on the tiled floor; Harry shrieked and the dogs barked again. As the boys scrambled to pick up the precious pieces the door opened and Susan Hodge came in in her dressing gown.

'What on earth's going on?'

'Look! Look!'

Jake laid out their findings on the kitchen table, where

he saw them for the first time in a good light. Having had most of the mud scrubbed off they did truly look like the sort of bits you saw in glass cases in museums.

'I found it with my metal detector! In Miss Brocklebank's veg patch – ages ago – we knew it was there all the time—'

He stumbled out the story. His mother, understandably, was stunned.

'What does this mean? Is it valuable? Is it yours?'

'Yes, yes! Mine and Miss Brocklebank's. That's the law. And there's lots more. We just started on it but we can't see in the dark. Tomorrow —'

'We couldn't dig it up until Miss Brocklebank went – the flood gave us the chance—'

'It was under her leeks. We had to pull them out. It was under the stable floor but Polly cemented it over —'

'We've known for ages—'

Millie came in, woken by the excitement, and shouted out when she saw the pieces on the table.

'It's true then! There's more!'

Their laughing woke their father and Susan went upstairs to tell him about the find and he had to come down, rumbling and grumbling, to see the evidence. Like his wife, he found it hard to take in the significance of the find.

'Looks like junk to me.' But he was aware of the pot-luck way in which metal-detecting worked, having given permission to various enthusiasts to work on his land in the past, although not with any success.

'But this is on the old girl's land then, not ours?'

'No, but I found it, that's what matters.'

'Eh, you're going to share it with us, lad?'

His father laughed. Jake was not sure if he was serious. He glanced at his mother and she was laughing.

'I think we should drink to this,' she said and went to where the sloe gin was hidden behind the beer in the back of the dresser cupboard.

'It's all underneath the vegetable garden,' she told her husband. 'She won't like it, the digging up.'

'We've been waiting ages,' Jake said. 'We've known about it for months. But she won't be coming back, not without a house to live in?'

'She can buy a new one, if this is for real. How many millions?'

They all laughed and Susan Hodge poured the sloe gin, twice as much for herself and her husband as for the children.

'We'll have to contact someone who knows what's what. And not to let the news get out, else we'll have visitors – what do they call them – nighthawks. They come when your back's turned and pinch it all,' said Mike.

'We can ring up the museum tomorrow, the curator. He'll know the drill, surely? It's not the first finding round here. There was one over at Appleton only a little while ago,' said Susan.

They sat round the table, turning over the muddy pieces, drinking the sloe gin and laughing. It was like Christmas. How rich was Jake going to be? Millie thought she was still dreaming. When she went to bed at last her final thought was they mustn't let Amy know about it.

'What on earth were Jake and Harry doing last night, scrubbing stuff in a bucket and talking about treasure?' Amy asked Millie when she went to feed the horses in the morning.

Millie's jaw dropped to find Amy in residence.

'How do you know what they were doing?'

'I was sleeping over with Dragon. I heard them. They were right outside Dragon's door. They woke me up.'

'It was nothing. They had been playing about with the metal detector and it beeped in Miss Brocklebank's garden – ages ago – so now she's not there they thought they'd have a dig. But it was only rubbish, nails and horseshoes and things.'

'They said it was treasure. They were really excited.'

'Kidding themselves. They brought it home and it was just rubbish.'

'Didn't sound like it to me. Jake said they were going to be millionaires. Who's kidding whom?'

'You'd better ask Jake. If he wants you to know he'll tell you.'

Millie was fuming to think the ghastly Amy was sticking her nose into their secret. And sleeping in the stable – their stable, hers and Imogen's. What a cheek! But then she remembered that Jake's find was a secret no longer and today their parents were getting in touch with the museum people and then everyone would know. She could not help tremors of excitement coming back at the memory of the night-time junketing with their parents and the lark of trying to think what they would do with a million pounds. Jake's million pounds, that is. (How he was going to keep it out of his father's hands was one of the things she really didn't want to think about.) Her head was whirling again now that Amy had raised the subject. But Amy was the last person she wanted to discuss it with. Change the subject.

'Mum said we've got to go back to school today but we don't know how to get there. How do you get up here from the village?'

'There are workmen down by the bridge and they'll take you across in their work boat if you ask. It's against the rules of course.'

'It'll take ages to rebuild the bridge.'

'I don't think they're going to. I heard them talking about abandoning this road, because it's not only the village bridge that's down, but the one beyond your farm as well. So they're saying they're going to make the traffic go out of the village the other way and right round, up to the main road, not past here at all.'

'What?'

Her father's dream come true! Millie couldn't believe it. Their road with no traffic! And a million pounds as well! It was all happening at once. But no bridge out of the village ... how would they get to school, go shopping? How would Polly get to her horses? She would take them away. They would be on their own again, without even Miss Brocklebank to worry about ... Millie's head was reeling. With the livery horses gone, no competition to get involved in, no ghastly dressage debacle to think about! What bliss! Just her and Imogen and how it all was before Polly ... a little sliver of her mind said how boring, but she dismissed it.

'We'll be cut off.'

'They're making a footbridge, they said. Just for people.'

'Polly won't be able to drive here. She'll never walk.'

'She can drive the back way, as far as Standing Hall. And walk the last bit. Down through the woods and over the footbridge.'

Their footbridge was still standing, strangely, even with Miss Brocklebank's cottage destroyed.

'Her arena's floated away.'

Millie felt as if her brain had floated away too, so much had changed in the last twenty-four hours. She fed the horses and Bluebell and Barney and went out and stood looking at the river, trying to digest Amy's bombshells. The river now looked benign, as if it had never gone mad and nearly drowned them all. It was hardly swollen, and the ford was passable, the footbridge well clear of the water. The fields were all showing again, squelchy and rather untidy with tree debris scattered, but they were fields again, not a brimming lake. Down by the village JCBs were removing the bridge remains out of the water. They were the only source of traffic noise for none came from the road. The museum people would not be able to gain access.

But she reckoned without their excitement. They came, fully kitted out with gumboots and food. She told her father what she had heard about the road being abandoned and another bottle of sloe wine was drunk. Jake did not go to school, showing the museum people his site, nor did Millie. Harry and Imogen came down; Amy went off on Dragon. Later Polly and Joe and Alex turned up and discussed their situation, sitting on the feed-bins and smoking (in spite of Polly's own notices saying not to); the museum people came in to eat their sandwiches and they all got chatting together. They had a problem they shared: of how to get access to the stable yard now there were no bridges. Harry and Jake, hanging around listening, told them there was access if they had four-wheeled drive via a track from the back of the farm cattle sheds which went across the fields away from the farm to the outlying main road.

'Dad hardly ever uses it in that direction, only the bit to and from the house, so it's pretty rough,' Jake said. 'But it's the only way out for us now, so I suppose it will have to be improved.'

'The council will have to do it.'

'Or we can't go to school.'

Millie asked Polly if she had seen the lady of Standing Hall but Polly said gloomily the lady was in Italy for the winter and the prospect of moving there in the near future seemed remote.

'It looks as if we shall just have to make do with here for the time being.'

Millie was piqued by the implied insult and said indignantly, 'We told you it flooded. You didn't listen.'

'Well, there are floods and floods. You never said the horses would drown, only get their feet wet.'

'It's never done that before. Never.'

'Well, let's hope never again. Not while we're here anyway.'

And while she was arguing with Polly, Millie thought of something else.

'Do you know what's happened to Miss Brocklebank, your poor old auntie? Is she okay?'

If she knew what was happening to her garden she wouldn't be. The museum archaeologists had made in one day a digging that had destroyed nearly all the garden and great tracts of the field beyond. The place looked terrible. If Miss Brocklebank were to see it she would die.

And if she died half the millions would go to Polly!

Millie's jaw dropped down at the sudden realisation. She was struck dumb.

Polly said carelessly, 'She's been taken somewhere, I'm not sure where. I suppose I ought to do something about it.'

Millie wanted to kill her. She ran all the way home and told her mother that if Miss Brocklebank died Polly would get all the money.

'Surely Polly is going to find her somewhere to live? I assumed the old girl was in good hands.'

'Polly doesn't even know where she is!'

'Oh my word, that's dreadful! I must do something about it. I'll ring up the council offices. Someone there should know. If the worst comes to the worst the old girl can come here while somebody finds her a new place.'

'She mustn't die!'

That was the family mantra as soon as they all realised the horror of Polly inheriting what was proving to be a considerable treasure hoard. The archaeologists came every day, set up camp in the stable yard, appropriated the barns, established a night-watch. The story was in all the newspapers; the television people came – or tried to come but their vans got bogged down behind Mike Hodge's cattle sheds, much to his delight. He pulled them out with his tractor but they decided not to come any further. Susan Hodge discovered Miss Brocklebank in the council's old people's home and immediately contacted Polly to find her a new home. But Miss Brocklebank said she liked the old people's home because it had nearly an acre of garden in a shocking state and all she wanted were her own garden tools so that she could get started on repairing it.

'Her eyes were positively shining at the prospect,' Susan told Millie. 'She's being well fed for the first time in her life, she's warm and comfortable and she looks twice the poor thing she was before the flood. There's no way she's going to die, not with that old garden to bring back to life: it will really give her something to live for. Poor old Polly's going to have to wait.'

'Jake's used to digging. He can take her tools up there, if he can find them, and do the heavy stuff for her,' Mike Hodge decided.

The council had improved the back track out of his cattle sheds and it was now their way to get to the village, although a long way round. Harry found someone with a dinghy for sale and they bought it and used it to cross the river to the village to go backwards and forwards to school. Jake was now something of a celebrity. A schoolboy with a fortune!

'Everyone wants to be friends with me,' he said. 'Even the teachers.'

The archaeologists had not finished digging but had already estimated the value of the find somewhere near a million or possibly a lot more.

The fact had sunk in slowly in the family circle. It still didn't have much reality, in that no one could see how it would change anything. There was nothing they wanted changed, not the farm, nor their way of life, not even school.

'What would we do without the farm?' Mike said. 'Watch telly all day? I've got my wish – the road gone. That's worth a million pounds to me any day.'

Jake remarked that he had no intention of putting his father into retirement. The money was his.

'You can't spend it, lad. It'll have to be put away,' said his father. 'Unless you'd like to buy me a new tractor,' he added.

'We could all have presents, surely? I could buy Millie a decent pony for a start instead of that spotted weed, one that will do perfect dressARGE so that she can stop worrying about this stupid competition.'

'I don't want another pony!' Millie was enraged by the aspersions he was casting on her beloved Bluebell. 'The competition doesn't matter!'

'You could fool me.'

'Millie has to have something to worry about. It's her nature,' said her mother.

'Of course the competition doesn't matter. Although it would be nice to beat that stuck-up Polly Power. Not bothering about her poor old auntie indeed! Yes, Millie, you must beat Polly.'

'But it means working with Amy and that idiot Alex!'

'Good practice for life, my dear, working with people who drive you mad.'

Her mother grinned at her husband and he, happy for once, laughed.

Chapter 14

The competition wasn't going to go away, Millie could see, as Imogen was now set madly on making their input something to outshine the two stars to whom they were to be subservient.

'They don't even care what we do – just jiggle about indeed! – in the background while they do all the clever stuff. No way! We'll train our two to do something stunning, but quietly, in the background.'

'And how do we do that?'

'Out of that book I showed you, *Classical Circus Equitation*, the one I got out of the skip.'

'It's supposed to be dressage, not a circus.'

'Well, if Dragon's going to be dressed as a bull and Alex's planning to look like a matador it sounds more like circus to me than dressage. They've only invited us to participate because they're sorry for us with our two useless ponies.'

'You mean they're just being kind?'

'Yes, of course. We just stand there, dressed like nitwits, in no way to outshine Alex and Amy. Poor Barney and Bluebell. They don't want anybody to notice us. But we can still do something clever, quietly.'

'Steal their thunder, you mean?'

'Mmm. Background stuff.' Imogen considered. 'We could teach them to lie down and then sit on them like spectators, watching Amy and Alex making fools of themselves. That would be quiet, in the background, what they want us to do.'

'That would be very clever, teaching them to lie down.'

'Yes and when we all leave the ring we could teach them to turn round and bow to the crowd. How about that?'

'Yes, but—'

'But – but – oh, you are so *negative*!' Imogen shouted at her.

Millie went off for a ride on her own, fed up. All she required of life was this … just ambling along up the hill and through the woods and being her own person, not having anything to worry about. Bluebell was such a sweetie, as undemanding as herself: he didn't want to be a show-jumper or a dressage show-off. He was so willing for her, not a bit stodgy, but never wanting to take off like the dreadful Dragon. She could take in everything around her, the first signs of spring in the air, the birds carolling madly from the treetops, the first primroses beginning to unroll, catkins in flower where the hazels crowded the path, Bluebell taking a snatch at the bright leaves … it all healed her perturbed spirit. Everything had been so crazy the last few weeks, and Imogen calling her negative hurt. She hadn't been negative the night of the flood when they had so nearly rescued Miss Brocklebank, she thought: Imogen could have done no better. Now she just wished things were back like they had been before Polly, when it was just themselves and the boys pottering around, the place to themselves. Negative, yes. How she liked it.

Jake was in a very good mood these days, not unnaturally, and was quite patient when she moaned to him about Polly and the competition. He had taken Miss Brocklebank's situation to heart and went up with Harry to the old people's home to clear the overgrown garden. They enjoyed doing a demolition job.

'The carers bring us out cups of tea and biscuits. They all think it's wonderful getting a new garden and old Miss B has got it all mapped out, even an asparagus bed. She's going to feed the whole house. It's great. She hasn't once enquired about the old place here, not about the stables or the leeks or anything. I told her about the find but she wasn't even interested. All she thinks about is buying seeds and getting on with it. Her room is piled high with seed catalogues and special offers out of newspapers and new wellies and things. She's as barmy as ever.'

'Well, in a good way. It's a new life for her. It'll keep her going for years.'

When she came back to the problem of the competition Jake said she could look it all up on the internet.

'What do you mean?'

'How to make horses lie down and bow and stuff. It tells you how to do it. It's all there.'

'What? Imogen's got it in some old book she got out of a skip.'

'Well, it's better to see it done on film.'

'Show me.'

Millie was not as nosy on the computer as Jake, who spent hours researching every idea that came into his head. It never occurred to her to Google 'how to make a horse lie down' or 'how to make a horse bow'. And there it all was, in video, with demonstrations. She watched as Jake clicked the different boxes and brought up all manner of weird animals lying down (or not) to the instructions of feisty girls.

'They're all American.'

'Yeah, they're crazier than English girls. Look, here's a horse that plays croquet and blows a trumpet.'

'No, let's see bowing.'

It looked quite easy. Millie studied all the different images intently. It seemed you had to feed the animal with titbits between its front legs, gradually drawing the titbit further and further back until the horse went down on one knee to get at it, at the same time saying 'Down.' Lying down was fairly similar, lifting a foreleg and giving the horse a shove so that it went over, not very sophisticated. None of the horses looked much like Red Sky. Millie couldn't somehow see any of this working with Red Sky. But with amiable Bluebell and Barney ... they would fall over in return for a carrot, she was sure. It made the whole prospect of taking part in the competition much rosier.

'I'm sure we could do that.'

Unless, of course, Google never showed the videos of the horses that wouldn't do it. That was quite likely, she thought … however, not to be negative. She told Imogen. Imogen was quite put out that she hadn't thought to look on Google. She looked.

'Yeah, fantastic.'

'It's not really dressage.'

'Well, it's like Alex said, his idea is entertainment. Some of the other competitors only ride round in circles and do cross-overs and suchlike to music. We've no idea what he's planning.'

'We'd better find out.'

'We'll ask him.'

They cornered Alex one evening when he came to ride Sultan, or Sultana as she was now more usually called. He didn't – like most males – care for grooming and tack cleaning but rode happily on a mud-encrusted white mare, usually without a hat, his blonde curls flying free. He really was rather delicious but such an idiot, the girls thought.

'What's this thing you're roping us in for, the competition? We need to know.'

'Don't worry. Your part is very minor, perfectly suitable for your little ponies. Amy and I are the bull and the matador in the ring, fighting – all eyes will be on us – and you just have to represent the spectators, shout 'Olé!', nothing difficult. It's to the music of *Carmen* – you know that? 'Tor-e-a-dor, di dadi-dadi-da—'

He burst into song, familiar enough.

'We just shout "Olé!"?'

'Yes, not at all taxing.'

'And what do Bluebell and Barney do?'

'Just stand there.'

'With us sitting on them shouting "Olé!"'

'You've got it.'

'I think we can manage that,' said Imogen, po-faced.

'Olé!' said Millie.

When he had gone they collapsed into giggles. From then on, every utterance was preceded by 'Olé!'

'Olé, Imogen, let's start on teaching our ponies their tricks. Where shall we do it?'

'Olé! Somewhere no one will see us. We mustn't let them know we're into sabotage.'

Amy unfortunately went everywhere; nowhere was safe from Amy crashing past on the sweating Dragon.

One evening Millie and Imogen rode up through the woods as far as Standing Hall and pulled up outside the gates of the beautiful stable yard. It was quite separate from the house, behind it, and from its gates a wide drive curved past the walled back gardens round the house to the front door.

'Inside that yard would be a great place to practise. Shut the gates and no one would see us. Olé!'

'Are they locked?'

They had always assumed they were but had never actually tried them. Having heard that the owner of the Hall was in Italy, Imogen was confident enough to get off Barney and try to lift the big round latch. Much to her surprise it gave easily and she was able to push the gate open. They went in and closed it behind them.

'Hey, Olé! And Olé! again!'

'It's heaven!'

The mellow stone buildings surrounded a square of thick grass, once mown but not recently. It was much the same size as their own stable yard, but was completely free of rubbish. With the gates shut it was completely private and contained. It had – to Millie – a distinct atmosphere of times past, when it was a yard of carriage horses and hunters, all turned out to perfection. But now quite silent, as if in waiting; the tops of the tall trees surrounding it waving gently in the spring breeze.

'It's beautiful. So peaceful. We could practise here. No one would ever see.'

They rode up there after school as the evenings grew lighter, and the others presumed they were just out hacking as usual. It was all go in the renovated arena, Polly drawing up a timetable for its use. She insisted on trying to teach Amy some of the refinements of riding but Amy and Alex were keeping their competition routine a secret from her. Alex came up on his days off from the boutique when he knew Polly would be in the shop. He warned Amy to be ready and she actually got Sultana saddled and bridled for him. Was she mellowing? No, not really.

'Come to sneer?' she said nastily to Millie and Imogen.

'Thought we were part of the act.'

'Oh, background, yes. Alex thought you would be cross if you were left out.'

'Yes, we would be. Olé! Can't wait to see Dragon do dressage. Never seen it done at the gallop.'

Alex came in first and rode around looking beautiful, doing fairly basic dressage. After his prelude, the music roared and in raced Amy on Dragon – yes, at the gallop. She circled the prancing Sultana, who was supposed to do pirouettes, following Dragon's direction, and then they came together and tried to do a fairly complicated 'fight', toing and froing in dressage sequences, finishing with Alex 'stabbing' Dragon, at which Dragon, instead of dying, set off at a final mad gallop.

'Well, that's stupid. He should lie down and die.' Imogen was not impressed.

'It's his soul, released, finding freedom,' Alex said. 'We can't teach him to lie down. It's not possible.'

Millie and Imogen exchanged meaningful glances and both said, 'Olé!'

'Yes, you have to shout "Olé!" when I stab him. You could wave your arms in the air.'

'What, act? That's extra.'

'Just shout "Olé!" then.'

He was impatient with them, sensing their scorn.

'We don't really need you. You needn't bother if you don't want to.'

'No, sorry Alex – we do want to, honest. We'll do our best.'

'I'll see that you have nice dresses – you know, those flounced, flamenco sort. You'll look grand and the ponies can have embroidered draperies, very pretty.'

'To hide all their bad points, as enumerated by Polly.'

'Well, sorry, yes.'

They had to admit it was true that Sultana and Dragon were a very beautiful pair and their ponies were not. But it was nice, after all, for Alex to count them in. They tried to be gracious.

'He means well.'

'Olé!'

Jake said when his money was in the bank he would buy them both new, super ponies.

'I thought it had to be put away until you were old.'

'Yeah, most of it, but Dad said we could all have presents first. That's because he wants a new tractor and Mum wants a new car. So it's not fair if you don't have anything. You can have a new pony. And Imogen too, if she wants. And Harry and I – we're still trying to work out what we want. Then it's put away.'

'There'll be none left after that.'

'Well, they're still finding things out there. I think the money's going to be quite a lot.'

The archaeologists were rather underfoot, Millie and Imogen found, using the middle of the stable yard for their caravans and tending to overlap into their barn where they used the kettle and the sofa and spread things out on the floor. They also left a plentiful supply of buns and biscuits around to which the girls helped themselves. 'Fair's fair,' as Imogen said.

Having no traffic on the road had put Mike Hodge in such a

happy frame of mind that Millie found life a lot more peaceful at home. No shouting and grumbling, no more bad temper. Everything was rosy, apart from the thought of the competition. And whether she wanted a new pony ... both she and Imogen were doubtful.

'I wish they would grow at the same rate as us,' Imogen said. 'Even if we don't want new ponies we'll be too big for them next year.'

Millie for once decided that the problem could be shelved until after the competition. First things first. Teach the ponies to bow and lie down. She did not feel very optimistic, as most of the advice kept saying how long it took to teach these tricks and that patience was the name of the game.

'We've only got six months until the competition.'

'They're very amenable though. Not idiots like Dragon.'

'They like to please, that's something. They're a bit dumb; they do as they're told.'

It was true that their ponies were happy to do anything for a titbit, as if they had never seen food in their lives before. The girls practised in the stable when no one else was about, lifting up a foreleg and feeding the titbit down below on the ground, far enough back so the pony had a job to reach it. After quite a lot of jiggling about, both ponies learned to go down on one knee to get the reward. But teaching them to do it without somebody lifting the leg up first was more difficult: they needed to do it to the voice, not by manipulation.

'B-o-w,' they said in clear, slow voices.

Most of the sessions ended in attacks of the giggles.

Without someone holding the leg, the trainer grovelling underneath the pony's belly with the titbit usually got trodden on. The pony naturally shuffled backwards, so the other person had to hold it forward with the bridle – that didn't work as then it couldn't get its head down, so they arranged it with its back-side hard against the wall, one of them underneath with the titbit and the other standing in front saying 'B-o-w.'

'It'll take years!'

Imogen, the one with all the best ideas, wasn't as patient as Millie. Because she was close to the stable Millie came down more often and if there was nobody about she did a little practice alone, just a few minutes. Bluebell was the best, Barney slightly more stubborn. In the old stable yard with no one likely to surprise them they could have had longer sessions but, as little and often was the best way forward, it was harder to find enough time to go up there as frequently as they would have liked.

'B-o-w,' they kept saying in loud, clear voices.

The ponies yawned. They looked for titbits between their front legs and Millie and Imogen grovelled about underneath them with a carrot. They had to buy carrots by the bagful. They got as far as getting the ponies down there without holding the leg but it was a long way to get them to do it just by the voice. And without a carrot.

'We can't have carrots when it's the real thing. '

Little and often. Imogen got fed up but Millie persevered. Bluebell was better at it than Barney, or maybe better at it because he got more lessons. Millie was on hand and learned to know when Amy wasn't about. Although the girls tried (not terribly hard) to make a friend of Amy, she didn't want them and rebuffed them with sneers and rude remarks. It was true that Dragon was having a very good effect on her, keeping her off the streets, as Polly put it, certainly giving her a purpose in life, and something to love, but Dragon didn't teach her any manners. She argued hugely with Alex but he, strangely, was patient with her.

'Any normal person would have given up on her by now,' Imogen said.

'Well, you couldn't really call Alex normal, could you?'

'He's weird but nice.'

'And she's weird but nasty.'

'But we want them to win, so we must do our bit.'

Jake came into the barn one evening and said to Millie, 'You know there was a horse on Google that played the trumpet?'

'Yes?'

'Well, I found one, a toy one, in the back of the junk in my bedroom. You could try it with Bluebell. It plays very easily. If you just put it in his mouth and he breathes out it will make a noise.'

They tried it. Bluebell blew the trumpet and stood, goggle-eyed, shaking his head. He dropped it in the straw, then put his head down and picked it up again. Millie put it the right way in his mouth and he blew it again. He threw up his head and sent it spinning across the stable, then followed it and stood nosing at it curiously.

'He likes it,' Jake said. 'He's a musical genius.'

Barney wouldn't have anything to do with it, but Bluebell was obviously intrigued.

'There you are,' said Jake. 'Another string to your bow. He can play the trumpet in time with *Carmen*.'

Imogen was greatly impressed.

'That's terrific. You work at it, Millie. He's got to keep it in his mouth for more than one blow. Keep it going.'

They bought another bag of carrots and the summer crept on. Alex measured them up for flamenco dresses which he would make himself; Amy fashioned herself a great bull's mask with wicked horns; Jake and Harry were roped in to make a doctored recording of the *Carmen* music to use for the performance; Polly and Joe did correct and perfect dressage in the arena nearly every night; Emma at the Equestrian Centre was said to have a new dressage horse that would win everything it entered for and Bluebell was steadily learning to play the trumpet.

Millie longed for it all to be over so that she would have nothing more to worry about.

Chapter 15

'The thing is, it's only a bit of fun, Millie. If everything goes wrong it'll only make it funnier. It's *entertainment*.'

'Not if *we* get it wrong.'

'If we get it wrong, it doesn't matter one bit. If Amy gets it wrong she might have half the audience in hospital.'

Millie made a great effort not to show what a wimp she was. She knew that Bluebell could play the trumpet if he was in the right mood, and Imogen had – amazingly! – got Barney to lie down. Sometimes he did it when he was supposed to bow. The trouble was the commands Bow and Down sounded rather similar. Imogen hadn't noticed the problem until quite far on in her training. She tried to change Down to Die but Barney refused to co-operate.

'Die!' she kept shouting, but nothing happened.

No one else in the stable was at all interested in what they were doing. Alex thought they were only going to shout Olé! and in their full rehearsals that was all they did. So now Millie worried terribly that in the real thing Bluebell and Barney wouldn't think to do their tricks. Polly had helped Amy and Alex to carry out the part of the act where they 'fought', or tried to do proper dressage, and she had helped Alex to make a clever entrance at the Spanish trot which was very advanced and quite difficult (the horse lifted its front legs very high and threw them out, but moved very steadily). Sultana could do it for several paces, then she shook her head and lapsed into an ordinary trot, but Alex was so keen to make a big impression he had worked at it very hard. The act started with him coming in first and showing off, before Dragon appeared at the gallop with a great crescendo in the well-known music – Toreador! De dadi dadi da! Jake and Harry were sweating blood to get the timing right, so that the music liaised with the horses. It was true that the horses were supposed to liaise with the music but the horses had their own ideas, inevitably. Sometimes they did and sometimes they didn't.

'We're not going in for the World Equestrian finals, for heaven's sake! We're only amateurs,' Alex complained to Jake.

'Say that again,' said Jake rudely.

Millie and Imogen kept their heads down.

'At least we'll win in the dress department,' Imogen said.

The flamenco dresses he had made them were astonishing. They were long with trains at the back and had extravagant flounces from top to bottom, round and round, in stunning colours. Trying them on Millie wanted to die, and Imogen was entranced.

'He said no one would notice us! Everyone will notice us!'

'If he made these for us background people, whatever has he made for himself?'

They were soon to find out.

'Dress rehearsal tonight,' he commanded. 'Polly's got a dinner date in London, so Joe won't bother to come. We'll have the place to ourselves.'

Jake and Harry were rounded up and set up their equipment in the water meadow. No one could ever believe that such a short while ago the meadows had turned into an inland sea: now they were serene and beautiful in the evening sunlight, close cropped by the horses and fringed with bulrushes and meadowsweet. The river rippled gently beneath the canopy of trees on the far side where the thrushes were singing their hearts out. On the road, nothing moved, save a brace of rabbits.

'Hope the weather's like this on the day!'

Struggling into their flounces the girls imagined how droopy they would look if it rained. All the horses had been bathed and shone, spotless, not a speck of mud to be seen. Sultana looked fantastic, sparkling white, her fine mane and gorgeous tail lifting like gossamer in the evening breeze.

And her rider …!!!

He climbed out of his Porsche in the stable yard.

'What do you think?'

The girls nearly fainted. Alex was usually dressed in very casual clothes and mostly wore jeans even to ride, but tonight he wore tight fitting crimson silk breeches and white silk stockings, and a fabulous figure-hugging jacket encrusted with gold embroidery and sparkling jewels over a white silk shirt and narrow black tie. The breeches were embroidered all down the sides with gold and silver curlicues and the stockings too were threaded with silver. Over his shoulders he had flung a crimson cape, and his blonde curls were slicked back and tied in a tight pigtail. At his side was a long theatrical sword.

The girls gawped, speechless.

'Good, eh? I've really enjoyed making these clothes. Pity the dressage isn't as good as the clothes, but we'll do our best. Olé!'

'Olé!'

It seemed Amy had spent all day prinking up Sultana to match up her rider, her own Dragon easy to do compared with the white mare. Dragon's coat always gleamed with good health; he was so fit under Amy's hard regime. And when she appeared it was obvious she had made her own outfit herself: she was all in black, with what was obviously a hired gorilla outfit over her body and arms and legs, but without the gorilla's head. Instead she wore a black balaclava and fixed to it a really threatening pair of bull's horns. It was, in a quite different way, as impressive as Alex's matador.

'That's great, Amy!'

'We'll get the Oscar for costume, whatever mess we make of

the display,' Imogen whispered to Millie. Their flounces were quite put in the shade by Alex.

They had bathed Bluebell and Barney and done their best to make their ponies as smart as possible, but neither Bluebell's indeterminate coat of washed-out piebald nor Barney's dull bay-sort-of-roan were good colours to impress, even when clean. No wonder Alex wanted them in the background. It seemed he hadn't had time to make them any draperies, which was something of a relief.

'I go in first to the *Carmen* music, doing my Spanish trot – I hope,' said Alex. 'Amy keeps hidden, but you two follow and go to the far side of the ring while I do my first dressage lark, alone. You just stay quiet and watch.'

They nodded politely.

'Then the music crescendoes and Amy comes in as the bull, doing her thing, showing how fierce and wild she is. Then she closes with me and we do the clever stuff, dressage style – fighting like, but with passage and pirouettes and things. Hopefully. We're not terribly good. Polly says we're not to say we're her pupils. She's going do it properly with Joe first so we've got to do our best.'

'So while you're fighting this is where we wave and shout "Olé!"?' said Imogen innocently.

'Yes, that's right. And after we've done our clever bit I stick the sword in Dragon (it's a theatrical one – it folds up as you push it in) and he gallops round the ring and exits. Then the music strikes up and I make a triumphal exit and you follow on behind and that's it.'

'Olé!'

'It's very simple for you, so no problem.'

Imogen said to Millie, 'None of our tricks for the rehearsal, just dumb clucks shouting "Olé!" When we see how it pans out we'll plan our bit for the real thing.'

Amy brought the pristine Sultana out for Alex to mount. No

one could deny that she had made a marvellous job of the mare, but she took the compliments without a smile. Millie realised that Amy's role in the exhibition was a lot more full of problems and potential disasters than their own, and wondered if her sour demeanour covered the same doubts as she herself harboured. Not that she would ever admit it; she totally rebuffed sympathy. Sometimes Millie felt guilty that they had never made much of an effort to befriend Amy, but the girl was so unfriendly herself that it seemed pointless to persevere. Dragon was her only friend and he was as horrible as she was.

They got on, riding bareback and sideways because of the dresses, and went out into the field.

'You enter behind me and then go to the far side of the ring to spectate while I do my clever stuff in front of the grandstand,' Alex said.

'Grandstand? It's only straw bales,' Jake said.

'Think grandstand! Think big!'

They thought Alex's costume had gone to his head, but they followed him meekly to the place marked with sticks as the entrance. Jake and Harry fiddled with their machinery and as the grand march from the last act of *Carmen* blasted out across the field they got on Sultana's tail and followed her in.

'Go away now,' Alex commanded.

They rode obediently out of the way and sat to watch. Alex proceeded at his Spanish trot until Sultana decided enough was enough and stopped doing it; then he moved into a fairly tame dressage routine. Because both the mare and her rider were so beautiful it was quite impressive.

'Cue Amy,' said Imogen.

The music changed and Amy came riding in at the gallop, as predicted. Alex rode out into the middle and she galloped round and round him in ever decreasing circles, while he followed her progress by making Sultana pirouette so that she faced him all the time. The pirouettes were very bad ones but effective and

Dragon's wild presence was impressive. Amy had him barely under control but wrestled him eventually into a trot and ranged herself alongside the mare, at which they went into a dressage routine, toing and froing in the semblance of a fight. It was quite clever but not up to Polly's standard. The two girls could see why she had told Alex and Amy not to pretend they were her pupils.

Alex duly stabbed Dragon and Amy screamed, Jake turned up the music and Dragon set off at another mad gallop round the ring. Millie and Imogen decided to join in with wild Olés! and Alex shouted at them to join him. Amy galloped out and Alex left the ring waving to the non-existent crowd as they, presumably, applauded. Bluebell and Barney followed.

'This is where we stop, turn and bow,' Imogen hissed at Millie. 'We hope.'

Imogen laughed. 'Jolly good!' she shouted to Alex.

Amy was still galloping about in the far distance and Alex wanted to talk to Jake about the music, so Millie and Imogen called it a day and took the ponies back to the barn.

'Come the day – anything could happen,' Imogen said happily.

That was what Millie was worried about.

But Millie had never felt happier that summer, even with the prospect of making a fool of herself in the show hanging over her. Her family was quite changed since her father's bad temper had disappeared. She had not realised how heavily it had affected all of them, especially her mother who had become jumpy and cross herself. Now their parents actually laughed together and chatted like good friends and she and Jake weren't nagged at all the time about homework. The main reason for Mike Hodge's newfound good humour was the closure of the road, not the prospect of Jake's great fortune, but there was no doubt that the thought of the money, even if it belonged to Jake, was a comfortable sort of cushion in the background of their lives. The archaeologists tidied up and departed in July and the estimate for the money they would receive was somewhere in the region of one and a half million, half of which would go to Miss Brocklebank.

'What a garden she's going to make – just think of it!' Jake remarked. 'They can have a conservatory and grow tropical fruit – pineapples and pomegranates and things. All the old folk of Under Standing will be queuing up to go into the home.'

'Well, she's no intention of leaving. She doesn't want to buy a new cottage. She loves it there.' Susan visited her at regular intervals. Polly had only been once.

'That girl is a disgrace. Let's hope the old girl leaves her share of the money to the home, not to Polly.'

'Yes, Mum, you can get her to make a will to say that. Polly's loaded already.'

Polly was known to be making moves to lease the stable yard at Standing Hall. The owner had returned from Italy and it seemed was interested in the prospect. The Hodges found it hard to believe that she was prepared to abandon Miss Brocklebank's yard after spending so much money on it. 'After all, it's never flooded like that before, and is very unlikely to do so again –– what a waste!' But Millie and Imogen, not to mention Jake and Harry, secretly hoped they could have the yard back to themselves, like it used to be. The livery people still felt like interlopers, somehow, rattling in and out at all times, taking away their long-established sense of ownership and privacy.

'It's not that we don't like them, but they're not us,' Imogen declared. 'I hope they go to Standing Hall.

'And Amy too, with luck.'

'Yes, especially Amy.'

'Pity about Amy.'

Did they all feel guilty about Amy, Millie wondered? Nobody was keen to discuss it, the unease about their failure to make a friend of Amy. They admired her and were awed by her rapport with the high-powered black horse which nobody else had ever volunteered to ride, but she seemed to have a grudge against the outside world – perhaps with good reason, how could they tell? – that precluded any wish to make friends. She had not grown any more mannerly or prettier or kinder with the year's passing but now was a stocky tank of a healthy outdoor girl, strong with an intimidating scowl, untidy black hair and scornful dark eyes. The only time she showed any softening in her nature was when she was in the loose-box with Dragon and could be heard talking to him in a quiet, cajoling voice, quite unlike her usual tone. At least somebody seemed to love her, even if it was only a mad horse.

Of course, as Polly said, 'This act of theirs, expecting Dragon to do a beautiful dressage test straight after a mad gallop round and round the ring, is asking the impossible.'

So is asking Bluebell and Barney to do their tricks to order, thought Millie. But Polly didn't know about that. Only Jake knew what they were planning He serviced the trumpet for them and spent some time himself teaching Bluebell to blow it.

'You can get a whole symphony out of him if he's in the mood.'

'Oh rubbish,' scoffed Imogen. She was a bit put out as Barney wouldn't have anything to do with the trumpet. She was still trying to get Barney to lie down to the command Die, instead of Down.

'Anything might happen on the day.'

'Say that again.'

Even Polly and Joe were on edge, let alone the *Carmen* cast.

The evening before the dread day, after Millie and Imogen had bathed the two ponies and wrapped them up in some of Polly's fly-sheets to keep them clean during the night, and combed out their manes and tails and oiled their hooves and ironed their own flounced dresses which took hours, Millie went down to the stables to see all was well.

'This time tomorrow it will all be over,' she was thinking. 'And anyway it's only a stupid bit of fun. What does it matter?'

Alex was only doing it to show off, they were in it because he asked them to, and Amy was in it to prove that Dragon was the best horse ever and she the best and boldest rider.

Bluebell and Barney were happily eating their haynets and merely blinked at her when she turned the light on and went on eating. It was a beautiful evening with a fantastic forecast for the following day: the show was a sell-out and the whole village was going to turn out to see the local talent performing. There were agility dogs and pig races and the bonniest baby which was bound to be a much more vicious competition than their own stupid performance. Most people said that bonniest baby was a no-no these days but the villagers of Under Standing always demanded it, in spite of the aftermath of indignation and upset.

Millie said goodnight to the ponies, turned off the light and went out into the yard. The light was on in Polly's stables and she thought someone had left it on by mistake and went across to put it out. But when she went in she realised that Amy was in Dragon's box. She hesitated, anxious to retreat, but knew Amy had seen her. It was too rude to turn away. She crossed over to Dragon's door and looked in.

'Sorry, I thought someone had left the light on. I'm not interfering.'

It was the cautious approach they had all learned to take with Amy.

To her surprise, Amy answered her. Not even a sneer.

'It's all right. I'm just saying goodnight.'

'You're not sleeping here?'

They knew she often did.

'No. I'm going home.'

Very rarely did Amy tell anyone of her intentions, however minor. Surprised, Millie did not turn away but leaned over the door. She felt it was worth prompting further communication, seeing that it was so rare, so she remarked, 'Dragon looks fantastic. I bet he's great tomorrow.'

At this there was no reply, and Millie, seeing Amy's expression, had a surprising realisation that Amy was feeling much the same as she did about the day ahead: apprehension rather than confidence.

She said, 'I'm not doing anything really, but I wish it was over. Stupid, isn't it, considering we don't have to do anything?'

Amy didn't say anything for a bit and Millie supposed the conversation, such as it was, was over, but as she turned to retreat, Amy said suddenly, 'My mother is coming to watch. I don't want it to go wrong.'

'Your mother!'

'She's on her own again. I can go home now. It's all right.'

Millie took this in, slowly realising what it meant to Amy, that she was perhaps welcome in her own home again. Her mother's boyfriend had left her. There was a place for Amy again. Is this what Amy meant? It was so hard to read her through the wall she always built around herself. And Millie only had the barest knowledge of how Amy had become the outcast she seemed to want to be.

'Will that make everything better for you?' Stupid question, the answer was obvious, but it was something to say.

'Yeah. Might. Who knows?'

And Amy actually smiled. She smiled! Millie nearly fainted.

To her relief at this point Dragon turned round and came up to the door, pushing his nose at Millie's hand. She could see he wasn't intending to bite (unlike when he had first arrived) and she stroked his tender muzzle, her mind racing over the confidence Amy had revealed. Was she being witness to what might prove to be a huge breakthrough in Amy's wild career?

'That's great,' she said. 'Really great for you.'

A sudden rush of exhilaration at her own confidence in a l oving family life almost overcame her. Not to be welcome in one's own home, by one's own mother, was inconceivable. Yet it was what Amy was living with. No wonder she was so horrible to all around her, who had what she hadn't. What nearly everyone took for granted. Everyone Millie knew, at any rate. Under Standing was a mild and untroubled (boring?) place, after all. Dragon's stable was more home to her than her own house. And Dragon was a safer subject for conversation than Amy's mother's boyfriend.

'It's amazing what you've done with Dragon. I'm sure he'll be terrific tomorrow.'

And Amy actually said, quietly, 'What he's done for me, more like.'

And Millie went home, her head swirling with thoughts that were nothing to do with making a fool of herself on the next day.

Chapter 16

Next morning the stable was a hive of activity. Millie and Imogen were glad of their separate barn as they could hear Polly and her pupils all getting in each other's' way in the main stable. Polly was euphoric with the news that she had taken a lease on the stables at Standing Hall. Millie and Imogen were equally euphoric that they would have their dear stable yard to themselves again.

'I can't believe all that money she's throwing away! After all she spent down here, and now just leaving it!'

'We can put the ponies in those grand loose-boxes! Miss Brocklebank has quite forgotten us, according to Mum.'

Millie told Imogen about her amazing meeting with Amy the evening before.

'She was almost nice. I couldn't believe it.'

'It'll be a bit dull down here without Dragon.'

'Maybe—' Millie couldn't actually bring herself to say it outright: that perhaps Amy might stay?

But time for all that later.

Jake and Harry were in a state about getting the music right, keeping it in time with the rather wild fluctuations of Alex's performance, obviously a far harder job than the girls' spectating. Polly was in a state of nerves and driving her pupils mad with fresh instructions and demands. They had collected a huge pile of accoutrements to load into the horsebox along with the horses, and Millie and Imogen elected to ride to the show. They could hack up round to Standing Hall and down the hill past Emma's. The show was to be held on the football field on the far side of the village. Susan Hodge said she would take their dresses and Millie stuffed the trumpet down the front of her jersey. She didn't want her mother asking questions. Their ponies were clean and only needed a final primping, their manes and tails combed out, their faces dusted and kissed and then they were away out of the chaos in the yard, across the river and up the hill through the trees. The sky was cloudless and there was no wind and no doubt the football field was already filling up with its usual collection of hotdog stalls, tame owl exhibitions, plant stalls, ancient tractor shows, Our Little Chicks dancing display, Guess the Weight, Name this Teddy and all the other paraphernalia that turned out every year.

'It's not a big space, for Amy to gallop round,' Imogen remarked. 'I hope Dragon doesn't run amok. It's tons smaller than where we rehearsed.'

'Well, we've only got to sit there.'

Millie supposed, when it came to the point, they wouldn't try any tricks: Alex had demanded nothing of them save a few Olés. She didn't feel as frightened as she had earlier, having witnessed the professional Polly losing her cool in the stables. She knew Polly was set on winning the competition, to beat her rival Emma, but Alex only wanted to show off and enjoy himself. He had never said anything about expecting them to win. That thought made Millie feel much better. Dear little Bluebell was so obliging and both ponies had been bowing quite well lately, although certainly could not be relied upon. The excitement of the show might blow them away: they lived a very quiet life, after all.

Passing the Equestrian Centre they saw that it was in a similar panic to Polly's with horses being bathed and stuff being loaded into trailers and girls shouting at each other. Polly said Emma's pupils were doing quadrilles and stuff, all very proper. At least

Alex and Amy were something a bit different. After all, the inhabitants of Under Standing knew little about dressage and probably cared less, and too much would quickly bore them. Bluebell playing the trumpet was certainly different, should he co-operate.

Millie's parents had arrived with all Jake's and Harry's gear in the Land Rover, and had parked it in a far corner under a shady tree. The girls decided to make it their base, rather than Polly's horsebox that would have to go in the horsebox park along with all the others. Mike Hodge had never deigned to come to this potty show before – 'No cattle, not interested' – and his presence now showed how laid back he had become since the changes in the family's circumstances. He was sitting on their flounced dresses which didn't help. His wife shooed him off and shook them out and offered lemonade, and Millie and Imogen tied the ponies to the side of the Land Rover. The ponies didn't seem at all put out by the crowd.

'Bluebell's been through so many travellers' markets he's used to crowds,' Imogen said rudely.

'It's his sweet nature. He's a natural gent.'

They reported for duty at Polly's horsebox and explained where they were and were given a timetable of events. The horse event took place in mid-afternoon, after the dog agility, and they came in after Polly and Joe and before Emma's quadrille. Emma's own dressage exhibition came last.

'Make sure you're down here in good time. I won't be able to help you, I'm afraid,' Polly said. 'I'll be doing my show. You must be in the collecting ring while Joe and I are performing.'

'Yes, ma'am,' said Alex, giving a cheeky salute.

They could see he was dying to start dressing up. Amy was sitting in the cab fiddling with her bull's horns. Alex said they were very hard to get in the right position. If they were in the right position Amy's eye-holes were then too high up and she couldn't see out.

'But it's a bit late to do anything about it now.'

Amy was back to her scowling self. Millie wondered if she had been dreaming the evening before. It was a bit worrying about Amy riding blind. But not her problem.

The dog agility was being set up, the local boys' band was playing enthusiastically at one end of the ground and a disco at the other and the smell of hotdogs permeated all. The crowd was swelling by the minute. Polly and Joe got dressed in their dressage array and mounted their horses to go and find somewhere to ride in and Millie and Imogen went back to get their ponies. It was rather public for getting into their flounced dresses but they managed by pulling them on, shaking them down and then climbing out of their jodhpurs from underneath. They weren't at all practical for riding in. It was impossible to ride astride. In the rehearsal at home they had sat sideways on the ponies' bare backs and not thought much about it, but now they realised that unless the ponies behaved impeccably, if they decided to jiggle about, they were very likely to slide off. They led them down to the horsebox and Millie managed to tuck the trumpet under her armpit beneath the copious flounces. They went round the edge of the ground feeling rather conspicuous but all eyes were on the dog agility. Millie could see that the waiting was going to be nerve-wracking. At least the dog agility had attracted a big crowd of spectators.

Alex came out of the horsebox in all his finery and Amy came out in her gorilla gear and they unboxed the horses. Sultana looked calm and wonderful but Dragon was already in a sweat and looked anything but calm. Millie held him while Amy mounted, but it was impossible to see her expression underneath the balaclava. Millie was stunned by her courage, prepared to ride Dragon through the crowd to the collecting ring. She wondered briefly about insurance but supposed the show was insured for death and injury. She hoped so.

Alex's fantastic presence caused the crowd to fall aside,

gawping, as they made their way to the collecting ring. Bluebell and Barney behaved perfectly and Amy's amazing riding had Dragon in hand, although he was prancing and snorting and raining white froth all over his immaculate black coat. The collecting ring was thankfully quite calm after all the over-excited dogs from the agility had been rounded up and removed and only Polly and Joe were there waiting, looking extremely professional. Joe was looking white: apparently his old granny had turned up to see what she could make of him and had planted her shooting stick firmly beside the judge's box.

Emma's bandwagon was apparently, according to Polly, running late and was in complete disarray.

'Lucky for them they're last to go.'

Emma had most of her pupils in various guises such as cowboys and Indians, ladies at the court of Marie Antoinette, characters out of Disney films etc. all doing duos and quadrilles and herself heading the bill on her dressage horse but they were all getting tangled up in each other and still trying to find their way to the collecting ring.

Polly was eyeing Dragon anxiously but decided wisely not to say anything. Dragon was doing amazing dressage without being asked, a Spanish trot on the spot, lifting his knees up high and pounding the long-suffering turf. He found it hard to stand still. Amy released his head and took him off for a walk, but it was impossible to calm him. He was all over the place.

Polly said to Alex, 'For God's sake don't let her gallop in – she'll kill someone.'

But there was no time for her to worry about it as the announcer was calling for the dressage to start, and Polly and Joe rode away into the ring to do their show.

Millie now began to feel the needles of doubt, not to mention fear, start to take hold in her stomach. She felt rather sick. Imogen was looking grim, and Alex was watching Dragon and Amy with an aghast expression, realising suddenly that he was responsible for what looked like a charge of dynamite about to be let loose on the carefree crowd. But such was his eagerness to show himself off in all his glory to the crowd that he quickly turned away, forgot Amy and started concentrating on himself. It was his show and he was the star turn. Millie and Imogen lined up behind him.

The glimpses they could see of Polly and Joe showed that they were doing a classic and what looked like an immaculate dressage test, and loud applause followed them as they came out of the ring. They were both stirred up and bursting with relief and triumph and had obviously completely forgotten about the trials that faced Alex, merely shouting, 'Good luck!' and 'Go for it!' as he moved to enter the ring.

Millie and Imogen rode their ponies close behind him and Jake and Harry started the music, the entry of the Toreador, and Alex made his grand entrance at the Spanish trot. Sultana actually seemed to appreciate that she too was showing off as she did the best Spanish trot she had ever managed. Millie and Imogen parted from her to ride across the ring to take up their lowly places as spectators. It wasn't very far. Quite a crowd was sitting on straw bales behind a fence made of white tape and when Millie and Imogen made their first cries of Olé! several people took it up. At this Bluebell and Barney for the first time started to jiggle about and the two girls decided to slide gracefully off their backs before they got tossed.

Alex was doing what he thought was a brilliant dressage show quite largely in time to the music and Sultana was so elegant and graceful that it went down very well.

The music died away, Sultana came to a halt and Jake got the big crash and crescendo for Amy's entrance just right, so that Dragon appeared spectacularly at the exact moment. If Polly had shouted after her 'Don't gallop!' the warning had had no effect, for Dragon bore down towards Millie and Imogen at such a pace that the spectators behind them bundled themselves backwards in chaotic disarray. Millie and Imogen waved their arms to get him to turn and he shot round with such a sudden change of direction that any rider but Amy would have gone flying. At the other end of the ring another bunch of spectators screamed and started running for it but Amy wrestled him round so that he now faced Sultana. She came alongside and pulled up so sharply that Dragon skidded and then went straight up on his hind legs. This had never been in the rehearsal but it was spectacular, especially as Amy sat like a rock and got her weight forward so that he didn't go over backwards. The rear seemed to frighten him as much as it frightened the spectators, for he then stood still momentarily, and as Jake changed the music yet again for their double act of dressage, the 'fighting' bit, he went into the routine perfectly.

'Blimey!'

Millie and Imogen were so relieved they burst into Olés of joy and the reassembled crowd behind them started to take it up. It wasn't a very impressive dressage performance, nothing like as good as Polly and Joe's, and Imogen hissed to Millie, 'Try him with the trumpet.'

Millie fished it out of her flounces and put it to Bluebell's lips as practised interminably at home and instead of dropping it as usually happened he took it tight in his teeth and blew out a loud blast. Then, as if enchanted with his own skill, he proceeded to toss his head up and down, blowing hard with each toss.

'Olé!' screamed Imogen, and the crowd behind them started laughing and shouting Olé! again.

Whether Alex could hear what was going on they never knew, for at this point he took out his sword to kill the bull and waved it high in the air but as he did so the long blade flew off and left Alex with just the hilt in his fist.

As Amy was poised to receive the blow before galloping off again Alex, with great presence of mind, made a theatrical lunge and shouted 'Die!'

At this, to Imogen's complete bewilderment, Barney's legs buckled and he lay down, just as she had been trying to teach him for weeks. She was standing close to him and he flumped heavily on the train of her flounced dress so that she was pinioned to the spot.

Amy started off on her 'liberation of the soul' gallop, coming straight towards them. Imogen screamed and jumped out of the way and the whole bottom part of her dress ripped off, leaving her hopping about in her pink knickers.

'Olé! Olé!' shouted the crowd in glee behind her.

Bluebell went on tooting on his trumpet and Amy galloped on her way with her horns having given up the ghost and hanging down on either side of her face so that she looked like a charging elephant with tusks instead of a charging bull. She couldn't afford to let go of the reins to pull back the balaclava that was now blinding her and Dragon continued his flight round the ring and once more bore down on the white mare standing still with her mesmerised rider still holding the useless hilt of his sword.

But the prospect of imminent extinction galvanised Alex into action. He swung Sultana round with a perfect pirouette and as Dragon came up to him he leaned down and grabbed Amy's reins. Sultana, so perfectly schooled, bounded forwards and enabled Alex to pull Dragon to a skidding halt. The two horses stood side by side, tossing their heads, and Alex had the presence of mind to wave his hat in the air as if it was all meant. Amy pulled her balaclava off and threw it disgustedly to the ground but everyone started to cheer at her amazing performance.

'Olé! Olé!'

Jake turned up the music. Barney went on lying contentedly on his side and Imogen started kicking him in a rage, clutching the remnants of her dress round her bottom. Millie found she was laughing so hard she could hardly stand up.

'Imogen, remember – the bow!' she gasped. 'We've got to end it properly!'

Barney heaved himself unwillingly to his feet and Imogen started to see the funny side of it, now she had managed to cover up her bottom. Millie snatched the wretched trumpet from Bluebell's mouth and threw it on the ground, and they led the ponies back to where Sultana and Dragon were just leaving the ring.

'They won't do it,' Imogen hissed.

'Try it!' Millie hissed back. 'Barney died, didn't he?'

'The idiot!'

Alex and Amy were waiting for them at the exit, turned towards the crowd. As they reached them Millie and Imogen turned their ponies to face the ring and said as one, in their sternest voices, 'Bow.'

And as a perfect pair the two ponies both went down on one knee so that it touched the ground, put their heads down between their legs and each made a perfect bow.

The crowd roared.

'Olé! Olé!'

Jake cleverly turned up the music and the four of them left the ring.

Nothing made sense after that. Millie was so mightily relieved that her part in the fiasco was blameless that she was filled with euphoria: that there were absolutely no worries ahead of her, just lovely simple life. She stood in her stupid outfit, grinning all over her face. Imogen was wild about her dress coming apart and couldn't forgive Barney for lying down so inconveniently; Amy was shell-shocked and merely relieved to be still alive and Alex couldn't quite make out whether their show was a triumph or a disaster. However, having shown himself off so splendidly in all his finery to the crowd he felt rather good, and was congratulating Jake and Harry on their timing with the music which – when they all came to think about it later – was probably the cleverest part of the whole show.

Polly, who was still brimming with delight on the success of her own show with Joe, congratulated them in a rather roundabout manner, a dubious praise but still stipulating that they were to make it clear that they were not her pupils.

'I'm a dressage instructor, not a circus trainer.'

Emma, waiting to go on her high-powered dressage horse while her pupils were getting into serious tangles before they had even entered the ring, snapped, 'How you could allow Amy out in public on that dangerous horse is beyond me. It's lucky no one was killed.'

'Amy is not a pupil of mine. She keeps her horse in my stable but what she does with it is her own affair. According to you, that horse was unrideable, so she must be doing something right.'

'The horse is mad and so is the girl.'

By inference so was Polly.

When she rode off Polly said tightly, 'If we don't beat her I shall give up. Go in for tennis – water-skiing – anything—'

'Oh, you'll win easily,' said Alex airily. 'We'll be bottom, but it was great fun. And the ponies bowing was fantastic. A real surprise. They kept it a secret, I never knew. Fantastic!'

Everyone was saying the same, really impressed as they waited for Susan Hodge to fetch Imogen's jodhpurs to make her decent before going back to the horsebox. Joe was summoned by an imperious old lady amongst the spectators and rode over to greet his granny with a look on his face as if summoned to the headmaster's office for smoking behind the bike shed and Amy, walking Dragon round to try to unwind him, was approached by a tough-looking, black-haired woman who ducked under the rope and stalked towards her. Amy pulled up. The woman shouted, 'Hi, kid. I thought you were a goner! That bloody horse'll kill you sooner or later.'

'No, Mum, he was great.'

'You could fool me!'

Dragon wanted to move on so Amy walked away and the woman went with her, yakking away, so Millie didn't hear any more conversation. But she heard Amy laugh. The first time ever. She was stunned.

Imogen's jodhpurs arrived and she made herself respectable and they all trailed back to the horsebox. The crowd made way for them, laughing and shouting compliments, and even if they were going to be bottom they all felt great. They couldn't see Emma's display from the horsebox but heard outbursts of clapping, which made Polly clench her teeth.

'You're going to win, darling, don't worry,' Alex told her.

Joe, returning from his interview with his granny, brought out a bottle of champagne and a stack of cardboard cups.

'She thinks I'm great! She loves me! Let's drink now, before the results. Make us all happy.'

Millie thought he needed strong drink, having suffered Polly's instruction for so long and now no doubt looking forward to a rest. Even if he hadn't wanted it, she saw that he had a friend in his gentle, generous horse Wake. If Polly had chosen Wake for him she had certainly done him a good turn. Funny, she thought, they all had horses that suited them: pretty, coquettish Sultana for pretty, sweet Alex; sharp, snappy Red Sky for sharp, snappy Polly; tough, dangerous Dragon for wild, inscrutable Amy. Bluebell and Barney for herself and Imogen … she couldn't quite work out what that meant …

Amy joined them in time for the champagne.

Polly raised her drink and proposed the toast. 'Here's to us for all doing a jolly good show!'

They all drank. Amy choked and Millie started to sneeze and couldn't stop.

Polly ignored them and continued: 'And here's to our future in Standing Hall. I've signed a lease with the old girl and it's all settled. We move next week. And here's thank you to Millie and Imogen and Jake and Harry for putting up with us for so long.'

Millie choked some more, and even Imogen started snorting with surprise. Next week they were thinking! Peace at last! More champagne! They all started talking at once, as Polly's news was a surprise to everyone, and only stopped when an announcement came over the loudspeaker:

'The judges now have the results of the dressage competition.'

The crowd went silent, and the champagne drinkers all froze.

The voice continued: 'We found it very difficult to come to a decision as it seemed to us that we were confronted with skill of a very high order and as well with a high degree of entertainment. Although we know, strictly speaking, the prize should go to the most skilled, we thought that the winner should be the entry that most entertained the happy crowd that we have here today. Therefore we are awarding first prize to the *Carmen* bullfighting entry, and second prize to the Polly Power dressage duo. Please come into the ring and receive your awards.'

Having beaten Emma, Polly's tight face broke into a gasp of delight, while the *Carmen* bullfighting entry stood astonished with their champagne cups still raised. Alex was thrilled, Millie struck dumb, and Imogen moaned, 'I can't go into the ring looking like this!' She was still flounced at the top and did look extremely odd.

'Go on, it's part of the entertainment,' Jake told her.

So they got a leg up to sit sideways on Bluebell and Barney and Alex led them into the ring with Amy at his side. Polly and Joe followed. The crowd roared. Alex was loving every minute of glory and Sultana did some Spanish trot unasked, as big a show-off as her rider. Dragon was all ready to go straight into a gallop again, and Amy as usual had her hands full keeping him calm. But she sat so calmly herself and handled him with such skill that the knowledgeable in the crowd gave her a round of genuine applause as she followed Alex round the ring. Millie and Imogen managed to stay on board but reached the exit with great relief.

'Let's not bow again!' Millie hissed. 'They're bound to get it wrong.'

'No. Enough is enough.'

Amy's mother was prancing about by the exit, yelling 'Good on yer, Amy! Great stuff!'

She would have made an excellent bull herself, Millie thought, a larger tank-like being than her daughter, and obviously not one to cross. It made Millie laugh to see Amy laugh at her mother – what a pair! But a relief – such a relief – to know now that they were back to having their dear old stable yard to themselves again. Polly's pronouncement had been a shock, a wonderful shock.

She rode back to her parents' Land Rover with Imogen, both of them laughing at the shock of winning. Her mother and father were amazed at the ponies' tricks and full of praise; a picnic was produced, the ponies let off on long ropes to graze and eventually the two girls changed into ordinary clothes and saddled up to ride home.

The sun was casting long shadows through the woods and it was a perfect ride to end the day: the path they knew so well down through the trees to the river, where they let the ponies take a long drink. They turned the ponies out and went home before the others arrived, not wanting any more excitement.

'Amy might be a reformed character now her mother's boyfriend had disappeared from the scene. Funny her mum turning up like that. Glad she's not my mother.'

Imogen set off across the field for home and Millie walked back up the hill, feeling glad of her own parents, who had enjoyed seeing their children make fools of themselves at the show. Amy's reformed mother had come to watch her daughter but Imogen's parents hadn't come, although they were not abroad or in London as they often were. Odd, Millie thought. People are funny.

Much later, after the excitements of the day and a hearty supper, Millie knew she would never go to sleep in a hurry, so decided to walk down the hill and say goodnight to the horses. All her fears were over: the show had been brilliant and the news of Polly's departure was fantastic. The place would be theirs again and they could always pick up the friendships whenever they liked by visiting up the hill, it was no distance.

It was becoming dark now and all the horses had been turned out after their hard day. Millie could make out the white shape of Sultana grazing with the devoted Wake in close attendance, Red Sky as usual on her cantankerous own, and Dragon grazing with the two ponies. But so much for her solitary goodnight to dear Bluebell: Amy was there talking to Dragon. Millie thought she would have gone home by now to her reunited mother but obviously habit died hard.

She walked across the field with her carrots for the ponies, unsure as always how to approach Amy. But Amy appeared to be in much the same relaxed mood as herself, for the rare smile appeared as Millie approached.

'Dragon was great, wasn't he?'

'Fantastic. Great you stayed on. I never would've.'

'Yeah. Pity about the horns falling off but I got everything else right.'

Millie remembered the panic in the crowd as they all scrambled for safety at Dragon's approach, but supposed Amy had never doubted that she would stay in control.

'I'm glad it's over though. We never knew if the ponies would bow or not, for all the time we'd spent trying to teach them, but they did it beautifully.'

'Yeah. Alex was gobsmacked. It made a super ending.'

They fed Dragon and the ponies carrots, and Millie said:

'You going home tonight? Now your mum's on her own again?'

'Yeah. He's gone. It's okay now.' She hesitated and then said,

'I don't want to go up there with Polly and them. I'd rather stay here.'

Her voice was questioning, rather pathetic. She was so used to being not wanted, Millie realised. Floored by the suggestion, Millie didn't know how to answer.

'Well ...'

Her mind raced: what would Imogen have to say about it? What would the boys think? It was their place too. The four of them had always meshed together in mostly total amity, arguing, joking, gossiping, rarely falling out about anything that mattered. But Amy, with her scowl, her gracelessness ... how would she fit in?

Nobody wanted her, only Dragon.

Millie prevaricated. 'I'll have to ask the others.'

Even to her own ears, that sounded unkind. Just when she had felt awash with a newfound peace of mind she was now assaulted by a far bigger problem than teaching Bluebell to play the trumpet. Her mind raced. She wanted time.

'Are you going home now? Shall I walk down to the bridge with you?'

'If you like.' Truculently.

The evening was so quiet, the first stars coming out in a deep blue sky, not a breath of wind, the familiar river smell drifting across the meadows. The defunct road was bliss; there had never been silence in the past, as there was now. They walked without talking, but Millie knew Amy's question was hanging in the air between them like something tangible, a cobweb of doubt. And as she went, passing first Red Sky and then the white mare and her companion Wake, Millie felt a strange confidence rising in her. Nothing had gone wrong today for all her fears, she now felt nothing but huge contentment with her life, with her friends, her family, her pony … so why was she so hesitant, so habitually nervous when it came to making a decision? What did it matter to the others, whether Amy was there or not? Still she hesitated.

They came to the river's edge where Amy had pulled up her kayak, the 'borrowed' craft she habitually used to cross the river. She wriggled into it and picked up the paddle.

'Goodnight then.'

'Goodnight.'

She pushed out from the bank and drifted away on the current. Gleams of phosphorescence danced on the surface of the water in her wake. Millie stared.

Then she shouted: 'Yes, Amy, yes! You stay!'

Did Amy hear her? All Millie saw was the phosphorescence break into a thousand shards of delight as Amy furiously dug in the paddle and spun the kayak into the centre of the river. Millie laughed. It was done.

She turned and started to walk home.